THE FRIENDSHIP SONG

Books by Nancy Springer

Not on a White Horse
They're All Named Wildfire
Red Wizard
The Friendship Song

THE FRIENDSHIP SONG
♪

by

Nancy Springer

ATHENEUM
1992
New York

MAXWELL MACMILLAN CANADA
Toronto

MAXWELL MACMILLAN INTERNATIONAL
New York Oxford Singapore Sydney

Atheneum
Macmillan Publishing Company
866 Third Avenue
New York, NY 10022

Maxwell Macmillan Canada, Inc.
1200 Eglinton Avenue East
Suite 200
Don Mills, Ontario M3C 3N1

Macmillan Publishing Company is part of the Maxwell Communication Group of Companies.

First edition

Printed in the United States of America

1   2   3   4   5   6   7   8   9   10

Book design by Marysarah Quinn

LIBRARY OF CONGRESS CATALOGING-IN-PUBLICATION DATA

Springer, Nancy.
    The friendship song/by Nancy Springer.—1st ed.
        p.   cm.
    Summary: Harper learns about true friendship when she and her friend Rawnie find their way through the underworld of her new stepmother's backyard to bring their favorite rock singer back from the dead.
    ISBN 0–689–31727–1
    [1. Friendship—Fiction.   2. Death—Fiction.   3. Orpheus (Greek mythology)—Fiction.]   I. Title.
    PZ7.S76846Fr   1992
    [Fic]—dc20   91–9483

To Joel, my husband and longtime best friend

THE FRIENDSHIP SONG

FOREWORD

♪

There were ordinary heroes, the ones with swords, and then there was the music hero, the one whose power was all for peace and singing. When he played his harp, the wild wolves came running to listen and oak trees uprooted themselves to follow him. He could lift beached ships back into the sea with his music, and make mountains weep, and calm earthquakes, and lull dragons to sleep.

Other heroes, the ones with swords, would venture to the world of the dead in order to steal treasure for the living. But the hero with the harp went there for another reason: love. The woman he adored, the love of his life, had died. He risked the dangers of the afterworld in an attempt to bring her back.

The king of the dead had cold eyes and no smile. Heroes were nothing but thieves to him. This one, the harper, came before him as a prisoner, his hands bound, his instrument hanging from his shoulder. As was the custom, the king told him, "You have one last request before we cast you into the shadowland where souls wander forever without rest."

The harper said, "Let me play one song for you."

They unbound his hands, and he played his harp so that notes flew out like silver birds. When he sang, the willow trees turned their heads toward him, the dark rivers of that place lay still and listened to him. After he finished the single song, he stopped, but the king of the dead urged him, "Play on."

"Grant me the life of my beloved."

"I will grant you, instead, your own life."

The harper played. His first song had been of courage, and this one was of joy and hope. The shades of the dead gathered to hear, hanging like mist in the air around him. The three-headed, snake-fanged dog that guarded the gates of the dead left his post and came and lay by the harper's feet.

When he finished the song the king begged, "Play on."

"Grant me the life of my beloved."

"I will grant you, instead, a circlet of gold to be your crown."

The harper played. This time his song was of sorrowing true love, and when he finished, tears were running down the hard face of the king, who could not speak.

"Grant me the life of my beloved," the harper softly said.

A shadow of self, she floated near him like the others, listening without recognizing him, for she had eaten the food of the dead and remembered nothing. The king lifted his hand, and she became solid again, and breathed, and clung to her lover and started to shake with fear, for she remembered everything.

The king found his voice. "Go," he told the harper gruffly, "and she will follow you, and nothing in my realm will harm either of you. But you must trust my word for this. Do not look back, or you will see her then and never again."

It is said that no one who has entered the afterworld and eaten the food of the dead can ever return. Perhaps the king knew the woman would never reach the living world, the hero would not be able to keep from looking back at her. He almost reached the gates, but then he had to look, he had to see, if his beloved was truly following him. When he turned, she screamed, melted into mist, and blew away, lost in the winds of shadowland.

Not many people remember her name: Euridice. But they still remember the harper, and say of him, "Orpheus wandered the world the rest of his days calling for her in song." They say, "Orpheus could make stars fall with the music of his harp and sing down the moon out of the sky, but who can get the better of that cold-eyed king?"

Now there are other heroes, other music, to try to get the better of death.

CHAPTER ONE

♪

The main thing I remember about the ride into the city is that Neon Shadow came on the radio and I turned the volume up real loud. Dad glanced over at me but didn't say anything. He knew I was way bad losing-sleep in love with Neon Shadow, and he knew I wasn't real happy about moving. So he just drove the U-Haul, and I just sat there listening to the hot metal music of the electric guitars and the way Nico's and Ty's voices melted together and the words they sang.

> *What we always been*
> *Is what we're always gonna be.*
> *When the first two fish*
> *Crawled up out of the sea*
> *And looked at each other*
> *And said, "Yo, brother,"*
> *Hey, doncha know they were you and me.*
> *We're friends.*

Friends. It was a nice thought, but girls like me—built like a moose and bigger than anybody else in sixth grade—girls like me didn't get a lot of friends. At least I sure never did. Okay, so I had blond hair and blue eyes, which made me a palomino moose, but so what? It took being cute to make a girl popular. There had been a few kids who seemed to like me, but no real close friends. And now I was going to have to start over in a new neighborhood, new school, new everything.

"That's a new release of an old song," Dad said when the song was over.

"I *know.*"

Usually he would have grumped at me, "Harper, you don't have to yell." But this time he just sighed.

I really did know it was an old song. *Metal Mag* said so. "Neon Shadow's nitro new cover of a rock classic," they called it. The name of the song was just "The Friendship Song." I liked it a lot. I mean, any kind of rock music gets me going, it makes me want to stomp my big feet and play air guitar, but this song—it was too good for air guitar, it was special. It really cooked, but it was want-to-cry beautiful at the same time.

I turned the radio down again to keep from annoying Dad too much. We were at the commercial strip right outside the city, where the Wendy's was, and the Taco Bell, and all the usual places. And then we drove past the Arena. The house, Dad's sweetie's house, was supposed to be near the Arena. So we were almost there.

Dad said, "Harper, you've got to admit a ten-room house is better than a little trailer."

I didn't say anything, because he was so happy

about what was happening, it made me feel bad for not being happy too. I mean, we were always real close, we hardly ever fought. It was just that right now everything was so sudden. Like, one minute he meets this truly strange woman named, of all things, Gus at a stupid art class, and the next minute they're getting married. So we had to move in with Gus, because her place was bigger than ours. But I liked the trailer. I'd lived there all my life, since the day I was born, practically. It was plenty big enough for just Dad and me.

"Try to give it a chance, Harper," Dad said.

"Sure."

"Gus is really looking forward to having a family."

What the heck was her real name? Gustavia? Augusta? Something gross anyway. And I wasn't about to be her "family." But I didn't say anything.

"The school district is a better one too. They offer Latin, calculus—"

"Dad, I *know*."

That was Dad, always worrying about me, always hoping I'd do better than he had. Which was why he had given me such a bizarre name. His name was Buddy. Buddy Ferree. "People with cute names don't get taken seriously," he'd told me once. I thought he'd done just fine for a person who'd taken care of a baby, me, instead of going to college. He was head of sales at Rugged Pak, a corrugated-box company.

"Here we are." Dad stopped the U-Haul at the curb. I spotted Gus walking toward us from—her house.

Oh, my God, what a freaky house.

Of course I should have guessed. I'd met Gus a couple of times. I knew she wore overalls and a baseball cap backward whenever she wasn't asleep. But it's hard to guess some things just from meeting a person. No matter how weird they are, you're still not going to assume they have a sixteen-foot metal cactus in the front yard. I mean, it was a thing put together out of pipes, and it looked like a cactus to me.

Gus said, "Yo, Groover," to me. She called me Groover, who knows why. But she kept on going past me, vaulted over the hood of the U-Haul, and went around to the driver's side. My dad had his window down, and Gus started kissing him.

"Ew, sick." I turned my back on them and got out.

Across the street there was a girl about my age sitting on her front steps watching Gus kiss my dad and everything. Wonderful. Just wonderful.

I meant to go inside the house and look around, but Gus's whole place was so strange I just stood and stared. All the other houses in the neighborhood were regular row houses close together, but her place stood off by itself with a big yard all around, and every inch of the yard had some kind of bizarre object on it, like a tower of hubcaps, and a claw-footed bathtub painted red and black, and a Statue of Liberty made out of venetian blinds. The house was all funkied up with pillars and steeples and things, and there was strange stuff hanging in the windows.

Just the same I would have gone inside, because I wanted to get dibs on the best bedroom, but it was like something took me by the shoulders and turned me around and shoved me away.

Really. It was just as if the yard or the house or something grew invisible hands and gave me a good

push. As if something didn't like me, which was okay
with me because I wasn't in any mood to like *it*. But
then again, it wasn't okay. What the hell was going
on?

There I was all of a sudden heading across the
street when I didn't mean to. And there was the neigh-
bor girl still sitting on a *normal*-looking house's front
steps and watching.

"Hi," I said to her, like it was my idea to come
stumbling into her face.

"Oh, hi," she said, pretending she hadn't seen me
before. She wasn't tiny, but she wasn't an overgrown
geek like me either. She was slim and pretty, with dark
hair and huge dark eyes and skin the smooth brown
color of caramel, and I could tell right away she wore
a bra. I was still hiding everything under a baggy
sweatshirt.

We both stared across at Gus's house. She and my
dad had finally got done sucking face and had the back
of the U-Haul open.

"My name's Rawnie," the girl said.

"I'm Harper."

"Huh?"

"*Harper.*" I hated my name.

"Oh. You're moving in?"

"Nah. We just stopped by because it looked like a
garage sale." Jeez, what did she think a U-Haul was for?

"Okay, dumb question. Is your dad marrying Spook
House McCogg?"

That was another dumb question. Like, Dad and
Gus were just chewing on each other because there
wasn't a McDonald's burger handy? But I let it go,

because something else seemed more important. I said, "Spook House?"

"That's what we call her around here." Rawnie looked up with eyes that flashed white, then moved over on her steps so there was room for me to sit down. So I sat beside her, and she said real soft, "Listen, I don't mess with her. She's nice and everything, but there's something strange about her place."

"No duh."

"Listen." She spoke in a hurry, with her voice low, like she was telling me something important and dangerous. Her eyes were like woods lakes, brown and deep. She said, "There's lights and voices over there after dark. And nobody goes in there with spray paint or anything, even though they do everywhere else. And there's this kid, Benjy Jacobs, down the street, he was missing for two days once, and when he finally showed up, he said he was in Spooky McCogg's backyard the whole time and couldn't get out."

"What do you mean, he couldn't get out?"

"He just couldn't get out! He said it was like there were spirits or something wouldn't let him get out."

I tried to laugh, but I didn't really because I was remembering a feeling like two invisible hands on my shoulders shoving me off the sidewalk into the street.

"Great," I said.

"Harper," Dad called, looking around for me like I was a little kid, like I might get snatched or hit by a car or something. That was the only thing that bothered me about my dad, the way he treated me like a baby sometimes.

"Over here," I called.

He saw me and beckoned for me to come help. He and Gus were finally ready to move stuff in. I got up to go, and Rawnie said to me, quick, "Hey, you need anything, I'll be here."

I just looked at her. Maybe she was trying to scare me because I had smart-mouthed at her. I mean, I wasn't happy about Gus, but I knew my dad wouldn't marry an ax murderer or anything.

Rawnie looked right back at me. "I mean it," she said.

I said, "Sure," and went back across the street to carry my boxes into Gus's house.

Gus went first and beckoned me after her, and I didn't feel anything strange sending me out of the yard this time when I walked across it to get to her front door. There was a knocker in the shape of a peace symbol on it. The inside of the house was as junked up as the outside, with all sorts of goofy things, like a brass bed instead of a sofa, and a porch swing in the living room hanging by chains from the ceiling, which was made of molded tin. And there was an old rusty plow blade done up to look like a sailing ship with copper-tubing masts. It sat in a huge bottle on the floor. Standing in a corner was some sort of metal chest with a big metal sunburst on its lid.

Gus saw me looking at it. "That's my coffin," she explained.

"Ew!"

"I don't want anybody ever putting me in one of those funeral home Dracula boxes, see. So I built my own."

"Well, shouldn't you keep it in the basement or something?"

"I like to look at it. Makes me humble. Reminds me where I'm headed."

I didn't get to choose my bedroom after all, because she had already cleared one out for me. Otherwise I never would have gotten my stuff in. Gus kept every room in the house full, with just a little path through the middle for people to walk on. My room was nice, the biggest one except for the one she and Dad were going to share. And it faced the house across the street where what's her name—Rawnie—was still sitting on her front stoop, watching.

It was Saturday. I knew that sometime before Monday I ought to go over and find out what grade Rawnie was in and ask her if I could walk to school with her. Dad wanted to take me, but I'd been telling him no, thanks anyway, but I could handle it. I didn't want kids to see me getting brought to my new school my first day like a baby. If I didn't have somebody to walk with, though, I might chicken out yet, because everything was different. Where I lived before was way out in the country, so I just waited at the entrance of the trailer park and got on a bus to go to school. But now I was going to have to find my school in the middle of the city, and I wasn't looking forward to that, and I wasn't looking forward to being there once I found it.

Rawnie glanced up toward my room, and I stepped back from the window. I wasn't ready to wave at her yet or anything like that, and I didn't want her to see me standing there. Probably she couldn't see me anyway. There was a big circle of heavy lacework metal hanging in the window. In fact there was some kind of metal circle hanging in every window in the house. Downstairs too.

"Whadaya think, Groover?" It was Gus, standing in the doorway, wanting to know if I liked my new room. Her face was pink, and she didn't perm her hair or wear any kind of makeup, and she had kind of a big nose. Actually she was big all over. She had monster feet. Well, maybe it was just that the work boots she wore made them look big, but anyway she was not much to look at, especially not in her baseball cap. My dad had dated lots of women who were a whole lot better looking than she was.

"I think you've got dirt on your face," I told her.

She just held up her hands, which were dirtier, and smiled, and came in. "C'mon. Do you like your room?"

"It's okay," I admitted. "What are those things in the windows?"

"Old heat grates I polished up. You know, from old houses?"

I didn't know.

"They used to put a hole in the floor so the heat could get up from downstairs, and they'd cover the hole with a fancy cast-iron grate."

"So what?" I sounded pretty rude, but I didn't care. Okay, so I wasn't going to fight with my dad about her, but that didn't mean I couldn't fight with *her.*

Gus didn't even blink, though. She pretended I was just asking a question, and said, "So what are they doing in the windows? Don't you think they look witchy? I like circles. Yang and yin and all that. But you can just say they're to keep what's outside out and what's inside in. There's magic in metal."

Ordinarily I might not have paid much attention, but after what Rawnie had been telling me, you better believe I did. I think my eyes bugged, and I said, "You serious?"

I would have felt better if she'd laughed at me. Mad, but better. But she didn't laugh. She just let her smile curl up around that honker of hers and shrugged her big shoulders and went out to get some more of my stuff for me to unpack.

I stayed in my room for a long time, arranging my stuff, partly because I knew I would feel better once I got my room set up and partly because I didn't want to deal with Gus or her house more than I had to. But finally I had to go to the bathroom, which was at the back of the house, and while I was there I looked out the bathroom window, and my mouth came wide open because I was looking down at Gus's backyard.

It was huge. Here was this neighborhood all full of skinny brick row houses with no front yards and only skinny little backyards running between fences to skinny little alleys. And here in the middle of everything was this big square wooden house Gus had, and its yard stopped the alleys and stretched clear to the next street.

And every inch of the yard was full of some kind of junk.

What I'd seen out front was bad enough, but at least it seemed like it was arranged for people to look at. Besides the cactusy-looking thing and the hubcap tower there was a tall metal spindle out front with octopus arms on top, and there was a weird-looking metal deer with pipes for legs and antlers made out of old pitchforks. Kind of lawn-ornament stuff if you were really nutsoid. But the backyard was like a huge crazy playground made of sheer junk. In between big trees I saw the usual backyard trash, like old cars up on blocks and old washtubs, but also cockeyed streetlamps, and old steam radiators, and a cookstove, the kind with legs, and a ton of other things I couldn't figure out through the branches in my way. There were sheds down there too, and a creek with some little ponds strung along it like shiny beads on a shiny ribbon.

My room could wait a few minutes. I ran downstairs and out the back door. Forget wearing a jacket, because it was warm as summer out, even though it was only April. I found my way across the first part of the yard to the water. I say "found" because it took some doing. I mean there were about sixteen piles of stuff in my way. But I managed, and it was worth it. The ponds were way cool. They were made out of a car-top carrier, and a fuel oil tank cut in half, and a concrete septic ring, and an upside-down Volkswagen body, and just about anything big and hollow Gus could stick into the ground. Most of them had goldfish in them. Some of those goldfish were the size of bass, and besides being gold some of them were black and some were pinto-spotted.

Once I had seen the creek I was going to head back to my room, but then I got just a glimpse of something big and bright red up ahead. You know how it is when you're around something really bright nail-polish red. I had to go see what it was.

So I stepped across the creek. But on the other side of it the yard was like a maze, even worse than before. Not a mess, not like a garbage dump—in fact it was real neat. But also real confusing. Gus kept a lot of her stuff either stacked under trees or else in lines with aisles in between. The junk was piled up so high that most of the time I couldn't see out of whatever aisle I was in. I'd end up going the opposite direction from the one I wanted. Or, really, not knowing what direction I was headed at all.

And sometimes I got the feeling that something didn't want to let me in.

It wasn't like hands against my shoulders this time, it was just a thick feeling, like when you walk into a room full of people who don't care about you. Even though nothing had happened to me I started to feel scared. And then I thought about what's-his-face, the kid who said he was in this yard for two days. If he was pretty stupid, maybe he really could have gotten lost back here. But maybe it wasn't just that he got lost.

I'd had enough. I turned around and headed back the way I came, and then—you guessed it. I couldn't find my way out.

I told myself that it was just that I had got myself in a panic. I told myself to calm down and think straight, but it was no use. I couldn't calm down, and I couldn't even find my way back to the creek, where I maybe could have lived on raw goldfish for a

week. I ran around that crazy maze for, I guess, ten
minutes, but it felt like ten hours, until I was all hot
and bothered and just about ready to cry.

"Groover?"

It was Gus, heading up one of the aisles toward me.
I'd never been so glad to see anybody in my life, and
also I just absolutely hated her.

She said, "Hey, you shouldn't run around like a
goofball in this heat. You're all red. C'mon, let's go get
some sun tea."

Being scared makes me mad, and being mad made
me open my mouth and tell her what I thought, especially since my dad wasn't anywhere around. I
yelled, "I am not a goofball! This yard is weird, and so
are you. I wish my dad had never met you."

She just looked at me with foggy gray eyes and
said, "I see."

She couldn't see, not really, or she would be fighting back. I mean, to me this was war. I stopped yelling,
but I meant what I said even more when I told her, "I
don't like it here, and I don't like you."

"I hear you." She wasn't smiling, but she didn't
seem angry either, which made me want to scream. I
wanted her to be angry, but all she did was say, "Have
you told your father any of this?"

"A little." Very little.

"Maybe you should tell him. Don't expect me to
do it. You can speak for yourself." She smiled then, but
not exactly at me. "Come on. Let's go cool off."

She led the way back to the house, and I had to
either stay out there by myself or follow, so I followed.

Supper was kind of quiet, because I wasn't talking any more than I had to. Speak for myself, huh. I'd never in a thousand years say hateful things to my dad the way I did to Gus, and especially not if she wanted me to. About the only thing I said at suppertime was that I was tired, which gave me an excuse to go to bed early. Which I did, around dusk. Before I got undressed I looked across the street at Rawnie's house, but I didn't see her anywhere. Not that I could really expect her to be still sitting on her stoop.

I really was tired, but for a long time I couldn't get to sleep, lying there in a strange room with my own yelling still echoing in my head and big stupid metal circles hanging in the windows. They threw weird shadows. I wanted to take them down, but I didn't quite dare, because I had the feeling there might really be something outside, and whatever it was I wanted it to stay there. I kept listening for noises. Sometimes I even half thought I heard something.

I did hear something.

Faint, very faint, like somebody playing a faraway radio, except—there was something about this music that wasn't like radio music at all. Something wild and wailing, something that made my spine chill. You couldn't put this music on a tape or in a radio or anything small. It wouldn't fit in that kind of box, and you couldn't catch it that way. I could barely hear it, but it scared me. I knew it was bigger than the world. I knew it was sending echoes as far as the stars.

I knew I had to be going crazy.

No. No, it wasn't me. It was this crazy place.

Next thing I was up out of bed, intent on tracking

down—what? A wisp of sound, so soft my own breathing drowned it out. I couldn't hear it once I moved, but I had a feeling it would be there again as soon as I lay down.

Finally I turned on a light and hunted around in my boxes until I found my Walkman, and then I turned off the light again and tuned myself in. Or out. Whatever. I lay in bed with the headphones over my ears, hoping Neon Shadow would come on, and after a while they did, and it was "The Friendship Song."

> *Friend, friend, friend,*
> *You're my father, you're my mother*
> *You're my sister and my brother.*
> *Hey, what we've always been*
> *Is what we're always gonna be,*
> *We're yang and yin,*
> *We're sun and wind,*
> *We're eternity,*
> *We're friends.*

What the heck were yang and yin? But I didn't care. The song made me feel that everything was going to be all right. I went to sleep.

CHAPTER TWO

♪

The next day, Sunday, I just stayed in my room pretty much all day. I had a lot of boxes to unpack and arranging to do, right? Right. I saw Rawnie sitting on her stoop in the afternoon, but I was too busy to go over and ask her if I could walk to school with her. Especially since she might ask questions about how I was doing at Gus's house.

All day till dusk I was too busy to even think, which was the way I wanted it. But then, just about the time the sky started to turn gray, there it was again: guitar notes the same pale steel color as the sky, and sounding just about as far away.

It wasn't like any music I'd ever heard before. You know how sometimes a rockabilly guitar player can hit the strings just like ringing a bunch of bells? It was sort of like that, but sort of not like that at all. Really it was more like hearing a wildcat snarling in the dark. If it wasn't that it sounded so far away I probably would have crawled into bed. I wanted to. What I was hearing made me feel shivery and cold.

I listened for about half a minute, and then I barged

out of my room, down the stairs, and out the front
door, which I slammed, and I stomped across the
street to Rawnie's place like it was all her fault. She
wasn't on her steps, but her door was open and she
was right inside it. She'd been watching TV, I guess,
and heard me coming.

"I'm not scared!" I yelled at her.

She just stood there staring at me, and who can
blame her? Here I was, charging at her like a moose
and bellowing like one too, and there she was standing like an Egyptian princess or something. With little
sparks of gold in her ears. She had pierced ears already. I'd been begging Dad for years to let me get my
ears pierced, and he kept saying not until I was thir-
teen. Rawnie had probably had her ears pierced since
she was a baby.

I made myself calm my voice down, and I said sort
of movie-hero style, "Look, we're going to figure this
thing out right now. Come on." I beckoned at her and
headed back down her steps.

"What? Wait a minute!" she said, but she came out
her door and followed me. I was in moose-stampede
mode again, so she didn't catch up to me until I was
back across the street in Gus's front yard. My front
yard now.

"Heather—"

"My name's *Harper!*"

She grabbed me by the arm to make me stand still,
and said, "Harper, what are you trying to do?"

Then she heard it too. I could tell by the look on
her face. She didn't look scared or big-eyed, the way

she was when I charged her. Her face just got real, real still.

"Wow," she whispered. "What's that?"

Thing is, what we were hearing was so freaky that sometimes it didn't even sound like music. Sometimes it sounded more like metal banging against metal back in Gus's junk collection somewhere. Or like tree branches complaining in the wind or maybe tapping against something hollow. But that was just on the surface that it sounded like noise. Underneath, it was music, it *felt* like music all the time. It went through you.

"That is what we are going to figure out," I said to Rawnie, quiet now. "What it is and where it's coming from."

"Okay," Rawnie said. At the time it didn't surprise me. I just sort of figured she'd want to know, like I did. But looking back now it surprises me a lot. Why didn't she just say, "No way!" and go home? She barely knew me. But she said, "Okay."

We stayed close together and started up the front yard, with the cactus and all the rest of the stuff looking down at us. It was starting to get dark, and the street lamps were coming on. Something threw a shadow on my face, and I flinched. "Hey," I said.

The octopus arms on the top of the spindle thing were going around. Each one had a bright-colored fan of metal at the end. "That's a whirligig," Rawnie said. "It moves in the wind."

"Oh." I watched it a minute. It was making a squeaking sound. "That's not it," I said.

"No."

We eased deeper into the yard until we were going past the side of the house. It had a big old porch all around the first floor, and I noticed clusters of metal tubing hanging from the edge of its roof, making soft dinging noises. "Wind chimes," I said. I guessed Gus had made them, because they were weird, like her, with freak-face circles for the pipes to hang from. Later I found out I was right, she did, but by then so much had happened they didn't seem weird anymore.

"That's not it either," Rawnie said.

"Darn," I said. We kept going toward the backyard, past some stripped-down motorcycles, an old gas pump with a broken glass globe on the top, some tall things that I figured out later were the skeletons of vending machines, and something that made me jump and go, "Aaaa!" It was a carnival dummy, the kind you might see on top of the funhouse, with its arms in the air.

"Lights up ahead," Rawnie said. Her voice quivered and she sounded scared, but she kept right on walking. So was I, getting scared, and I knew if she hadn't been with me, I would have chickened out and gone back.

The lights were strange, all colors but very dim and blurred as if they were floating in fog. The distant music seemed maybe to be coming from where the lights were.

We plodded toward them without saying a word to each other. Like a pair of zombies we reached the creek and stepped over. Still side by side, we went through the maze of aisles and piled-up junk, and with the lights coloring the sky to guide us, it wasn't hard to find our way. As we got nearer, the music didn't really seem to get any nearer, but I felt a sort of heartbeat behind it, a dark rapid pounding rhythm I heard more with my feet than with my ears.

"Drums?" I whispered to Rawnie. Whispering seemed like the thing to do at the time.

She just nodded. Maybe her voice wasn't working. I could see her shaking. The aisle was getting too narrow for both of us to go at once, and Rawnie slowed down and signaled me with her hand to go ahead. I didn't want to do it, but I knew it wasn't fair to make her go first when I was the one who'd had the bright idea to do this. So I went.

The aisle took a turn, and the next thing I knew, I was heading straight toward the music and looking straight at something big and bright red, and I stopped where I was. I lifted my hand to point, and I wanted to tell Rawnie to look, but before I could say anything a voice yelled, "Yo!"

I wanted to either run or faint, but I just stood there. Rawnie crammed herself up next to me, and we both stared, and there was Gus, smiling all over her pink face at both of us.

"Yo, Groover!" she called. "Who's your friend?" She didn't look the least bit mad or anything. Not that we were doing anything wrong, but for some reason I felt—I don't know. Like we were trespassing or party-crashing or something. Like we were breaking and entering and somebody might call the cops. I just felt really creepy about being there, and I was glad

Gus wasn't anywhere near us where she could get her big hands on us.

I wondered what she was doing. There was no way I could tell, because she was on the other side of the big red—car, it was a car sitting up on concrete blocks. A huge car, bright and slick, like red red lipstick. In fact, an absolutely humongous red car with majorly large fins, and Gus was looking at Rawnie and me over a sheet of plywood laid across its seats, over the top of where the roof should have been, so I realized it was a convertible.

I think Gus knew who Rawnie was all the time, because she just kept talking. "Isn't she a beauty?" I thought at first she meant Rawnie, but then the direction she pointed that schnoz of hers told me she meant the car. "She's a nineteen fifty-nine Cadillac Eldorado Biarritz. The jerk I got her from kept her under a tarp and made her rust." Gus made that sound like a punishable crime, then let it go. "But I'll take care of her. Isn't she something?"

I guess she was, because I'd never seen a car that big, and the shape of the fins and taillights made it look rocket-powered. But I wasn't interested in talking about a junker car right then. I said, "Gus, did you hear something? Like some kind of weird music?"

"Well, I'll be." She glanced from me to Rawnie, who just stood there looking back at her. Gus seemed kind of surprised. "Yeah, I did hear something," she said after a minute, "but it's gone now."

She was right about that. It was.

"You guys want to help me put another coat of paint on this baby?" Gus asked.

If she'd been working on the car for long, that sort of explained the lights. There were four big lights set up around it, strange-looking ones not on poles but in six-sided metal buildings made of tall pillars with funky metal flowers at the top. These things were standing in just about the place where we had seen weird lights in all colors. But these light bulbs were plain white, and they were bright, not dim like the ones we had seen.

Rawnie was looking at them too, and she took a couple of steps forward and asked Gus, "What kind of lights are those?"

"Nice, aren't they? Art deco. They're off an old bridge." Which didn't exactly answer the question, somehow, but at that point my father walked in.

I say "in" because the car and the lights were in sort of a clearing in the middle of the backyard and all its junk. For some reason Gus had welded together a few dozen of those old metal lawn chairs, all different kinds, into rows of six each, like big metal sofas, and they were in there too. They made it even harder to get around. Anyway, Dad walked in by another aisle, past some metal buckets and washtubs and things, like it was no trouble at all.

"Hi," he said to Rawnie with a smile. When he looked at me the smile changed into his mischief grin.

"Ghosties and ghoulies gonna get you if you don't scram to bed, Skiddo," he told me.

I felt glad to see him, and better because he was there with me, and mad at him, all at the same time. See, when I was a little kid he used to read me picture books, and my favorite was the one about the ghosties

and ghoulies and long-legged beasties and things that
go bump in the night. So when he wanted me to go to
bed, all he had to say was, "Ghosties and ghoulies," and
I'd scream and run. We made a game of it. But right
then I didn't appreciate it because, first of all, I wasn't
a little kid anymore and, second of all, I didn't want to
hear about ghosties and ghoulies when I was standing
in the middle of Gus's spooky backyard. I didn't like
being called Skiddo in front of Rawnie either.

"*Dad,*" I complained.

"Okay, earlies and schoolies. You've got to get up
tomorrow morning."

Why do parents always tell kids stuff the kids already know? It wasn't like I'd forgotten I had school in
the morning. Not hardly. "*Dad* ..." I wanted to tell
him I was not stupid, but then I decided to forget it,
because I had a thought. "Dad, did you hear music a
little bit ago?"

"Music? What kind?"

"Sort of rock music."

"Sort of?"

"Oh, never mind." I could see he hadn't. "Dad,
why does Gus have all this, uh, stuff?"

I was being a little rude on purpose, talking about
Gus like she wasn't there. Dad gave me a look. "Good
grief, Harper, ask *her.*"

Gus had come over to stand right by me. She didn't
make me ask the question again, though, the way she
could have. She just said, "Do you want the truth or
the excuse?"

The way she said it made it funny somehow, and I
almost smiled. But Rawnie was standing right by me,

and she didn't look like she wanted to smile, so I didn't. I said, "Truth!"

"Truth is, I like junk."

I probably could have figured that out by myself. Rawnie said, "And what's the excuse?"

"The excuse is, I'm a folk artist. Really. A guy from the museum came and said so. That stuff up front is art, and that makes me a folk."

She made a rubber-mouth face, and I had to smile. In fact, I laughed. Rawnie smiled too, but she said, "I got to get home."

"I'll go with you," I said. "Dad, I got to walk Rawnie home."

Gus said, "Can you two manage okay?" but we pretended we didn't hear her.

Even though it was dark, we didn't have any trouble finding our way across the creek. We didn't say anything until we were on the other side. Then Rawnie said, "Your dad's nice."

"Yeah." My dad really does put up with me pretty good, considering. "Except he drives me crazy sometimes," I added.

"They all do. You should hear my dad yell when I leave something on the sofa in the TV room."

I said, "Mine doesn't yell much, but he sort of hovers. Like I'm still his little bitty girl. He says he wants me to be something special, but how can I when he never wants to let me *do* anything?"

Rawnie sort of bopped and hip-hopped a few steps and said, "Well, at least he doesn't yell. I think he's nice. *Cute,* too."

"Uh-huh." He is. Dad has honey blond hair and a

nice face. I have pukey hair and pale weird eyes and braces.

We didn't say another thing until we were back on the front lawn. Then we stood listening to the darkness a minute. The music still wasn't there. I felt like an idiot, like somebody had made a fool of me, and I had a feeling it was Gus, but I couldn't be sure. I didn't say that. All I said was, "I don't get it."

"Me neither." But Rawnie wasn't shrugging it off. Her voice had turned soft and dark. "But it was right there, at that big car, before it went away. I know it was. I think it's got something to do with your stepmother."

That shot through me, because I wasn't thinking of Gus that way. "She's not my stepmother!"

"Well, what is she, then?"

"I dunno. Anyway, I'm not scared of her!"

"Yeah, I know. You're not scared. We already got that straight."

Rawnie had a smooth quiet face that just looked at me and didn't give anything away. I couldn't tell if she was teasing me or what.

I said, "Well, why should I be?"

We both knew there were about sixteen reasons, but Rawnie didn't say anything. She just looked up and down the street once, and then she said, "Well, I gotta go. Bye."

"Bye."

Then I thought, Jeez, I didn't talk to her about walking to school with me. But she was already inside her house. And I felt embarrassed to go knock and ask her when I hadn't even thanked her for—well, for anything.

And I'd already told Dad a dozen times I had it under control. Hey, I was so brave, I was just going to have to make it through my first day at the new school on my own.

Good going, Harper. Why did I always have to go and do this kind of dumb stuff? It was like I was trying to be big. As if I wasn't big enough, almost as tall as my father already.

Once I was safe in my room I listened to my radio again, but "The Friendship Song" didn't come on.

CHAPTER
THREE

♪

Next morning, whadaya know, there was Rawnie on the front sidewalk, waiting for me.

"Hey, hi!" I was really glad to see her. "Yo," I added.

"Yo, ho, ho," she said. "I hate Monday."

"You sure you don't want me to drive you, Harper?" Dad called. He was standing inside the front door, watching.

"I'm sure!" I called back, and I managed to almost sound happy because I had Rawnie with me.

We headed toward school. She didn't just walk, she did little dance steps the whole way. I'd already noticed she hardly ever stood still. Her feet were always moving, feeling out a tempo, like there was music in the air I couldn't hear. She had on a short skirt and a neon pink jacket and dangle earrings that swung when she moved. She looked terrific. I had on a baggy sweater and my best jeans, but I felt like a horse next to her.

I was glad she was with me though, because as soon as we got on the main street there were big kids standing on the corners watching us go past. Guys, mostly. Out-of-school guys with tattoos and wrecked clothes and a lot of attitude. I didn't look at them as we walked past, so I don't know for sure who yelled or if it was at Rawnie or me or what, but somebody yelled, "Hey, jailbait!" and "Hey, look at those hooters!" And then there was all sorts of whistling and calling, and they were laughing about something. After we got past them Rawnie looked at me like she was checking on me.

I said, "*Now* I'm scared." I was too, nearly as scared as I was out in Gus's backyard in the dark with the weird music going. I didn't know what the weird music was likely to do to me, but people tell all sorts of stories about what happens to girls in the city who walk in the wrong place at the wrong time.

Rawnie looked a little surprised and said, "You don't have to worry about them. All they're gonna do is yell dumb stuff."

"Is that all?" I meant it like, wasn't that bad enough?

"Yeah! School is worse than they are."

Oh, great. Just wonderful. Maybe she was trying to scare me. I should have known by then that Rawnie played straight with me, but I still hoped she was trying to scare me, because that would mean school wasn't as bad as she said.

It was, though. The thing was, if a guy on the street bothered you, you could go away. Or if he got too close to you, you could smack him hard or even kick him where it hurt to make him stop. But in school, you had to stay trapped in the same building as drug-heads or whoever. And if you hit somebody in school for something, you were the one who would get in trouble. I found that out before I even got to homeroom.

The middle school stuck up like another skinny brick house except six times as big. It looked too big to me, because where I went before, I was in an elementary-school sixth grade with one teacher, but now I was going to have to use a locker and go to different classes and everything.

There were groups of kids standing all around, and Rawnie steered me between them. Some she said hi to, and others she stayed away from. The "heads," the ones who looked a lot like the guys on the street corners, she stayed away from because they were the kind who would come up behind you in gym class and pull your shorts down. And she stayed away from the "preps" because they were stuck up. She waved at some guys who looked like real nerds and a skinny guy on a skateboard, but mostly we just talked to girls. They said hi to me when she introduced us, but even when I was talking with them I felt other kids staring at me. I wanted to just shrink, like a Shrinky Dink. I felt too big. Everything about me was too big.

Kids stared even more when I headed toward the door. Like they'd never seen a new person go into the school early before. But I had to do it whether they stared or not, because I had to get assigned to a homeroom. Rawnie went with me to show me where the office was.

I didn't get far, though, because practically first thing when I walked up the steps, before I got to the door even, some zit-faced boy ran up to me and said,

"Whatcha got, baby?" and grabbed at the front of my sweater.

"Hey!" I whacked him a good one, right across his pimples, to knock him away. There were some other boys watching and laughing, so I guess he did it on a dare. But that didn't help me any. They all ran, and a woman teacher with three chins had hold of me with one hand and Pimples with the other, and Pimples was whining, "I just said hi to her and she hit me!"

And of course I couldn't tell what it was really about. I mean, I'd rather have detention for a month than say he pinched my breast.

So there I was in the office all right, but not the way I'd expected. Poor dear Pimples had to go to the nurse and get an ice pack because my hand had put a red mark on his face, which I bet did not hurt nearly as much as part of me did, and I was supposed to see the disciplinarian, and I kept telling myself, I am not going to cry. Not. Going. To. Cry. Anything else could happen just as long as I didn't bawl. I wondered if they still paddled kids here.

They did. The disciplinarian, who was a big man named Mr. Kuchwald, told me that right away. Not on a first offense, but two more strikes and I was out. It was his job to scare me, and he made sure he did it. He showed me the paddle, which was big. He told me nobody was allowed to hit anybody in his school except him, and he said he hoped I was just off to a bad start and he hoped I was not going to make it a habit to come see him, and then he said, "Do you have anything to say, young lady?"

I just stood there. So far the not-crying was going

okay, but if I tried to say anything, it might mess me up. Anyway, I just wanted out.

"If you have anything on your mind, you say it to my face right now."

Just then there was a tap on the door, and it opened, and Rawnie came in. I could tell right away from looking at her that she didn't like being in Mr. Kuchwald's office any better than I did.

"Go out and wait your turn!" he snapped at her.

She stepped forward instead and said in a shaky voice, "I'm here about Harper. I saw what happened, and it wasn't her fault. He started it."

I think it took Mr. Kuchwald a minute to remember that I was Harper and to figure out that Rawnie had actually come in on her own to try to help me out, and I can't blame him, because I couldn't believe it myself. But while he was trying to figure it out he glared at her, and she looked about as sick as I felt. Finally he yelled at her, "You know the rules! I don't care who started it, nobody hits anybody!"

Rawnie said, "Mr. Kuchwald, he did something to her." Her voice was real soft.

"He did something? What?" But the look I was shooting her told her, Don't say it, and I think she was kind of choking on the words anyway. She stood there, and Mr. Kuchwald leaned toward her and barked, "You can't just come in here and make vague accusations!"

I had to get us out of there, so I said, "I don't want to get in fights. I won't hit anybody again, Mr. Kuchwald."

"Now, that's what I like to hear." He mellowed right away. "Tell you what. I don't like to give anybody detention on their very first day. You stay out of trouble from here on"—he had to look again at the paper where he had written my name—"Harper, and we'll both pretend this never happened."

Once we were both out in the hall again I stopped Rawnie with my hand and said, "Thanks."

"Sure." She sounded bitter.

"No, I mean it. Thanks for trying to help." I couldn't understand why she did it. Nobody had ever done anything like that for me before.

She looked me straight in the eye and said, "You don't have to thank me for anything. Ever."

I just looked back at her, trying to figure her out. But at least I didn't feel like crying anymore.

She said, "M, S, J," which means Majorly Stupid Jerks, and the way she rolled her eyes made me grin. And then I remembered I still didn't have a homeroom. So I had to go back into the office, and Rawnie waited for me, and then the bell rang, so we were both late. But we were smiling.

We had the same homeroom, so Rawnie could help me with my lock and locker a little bit before first period. But we didn't have the same schedule after that, so I was on my own. I was late to just about every class. Once I asked a big kid where I was supposed to be and got sent clear to the wrong end of the school. After that I just asked teachers.

I saw Rawnie at lunch, and she saved me a seat the way she'd promised, and her friends who sat with us were nice. The food was like barf, though. How could anybody, even a school cafeteria, make hamburgers into barfburgers? Maybe I was just so stressed out that nothing would have tasted good to me.

Maybe not. "Wait'll you get to eat the green hot dogs," one of Rawnie's friends told me.

"They're more gray than green," Rawnie said.

"So they're gray-green. You know what they're made out of? Processed worm guts."

Gee, thanks. Now I had that to look forward to.

I saw Pimples, whose name turned out to be Brent, in some of my classes. Brent looked like a head. I found out he was a bikehead, just roared around on his dirt bike all day every day he wasn't in school. And I found out bikeheads were supposed to be even more obnoxious than skateheads. Brent kept smirking at me, and if I had to look at him, I glared at him. When the final bell rang you better believe I was ready to go home. Altogether it had not been a real good day.

Rawnie and I walked back past hooting and stuff from the guys hanging out again, and this time I hardly even noticed.

"It was good you hit Brent even though you got in trouble," Rawnie said.

"You think so?" I figured one of two things would happen: Either the buttheads who went to that school would respect me a little and let me alone, or they would keep trying the same thing to see if they could get me in trouble again. I wasn't looking forward to finding out which way things went.

Rawnie said, "Yeah. I think you gotta stand up for

yourself. People in general, I mean, gotta stand up for themselves. And, you know, other people too."

I was too bummed to really hear what she was saying.

When we got close to home we cut through an alley, and Rawnie dawdled a little, bouncing through some dance moves and reading the graffiti. There was something spray-painted on every garage door, every shed, and every concrete-block wall. Some of it was serious, like SAVE THE OCEANS and LOVE AND ACID AND SMACK, NO WAY BACK. Some of it was funny, like MR. K WEARS SATIN PANTIES. And most of it was just plain gross. Some of it was so gross I didn't even know what it meant, but I didn't want to say so.

"See what I mean?" Rawnie said when we got to our street.

"See what you mean about what?"

"About your—uh, about Spook House McCogg. How come nobody ever spray-paints anything around her place?"

"I dunno." We were home. Well, it didn't feel like home, but we were there, in front of the house. "Well, uh, bye." I wanted to say thanks to Rawnie, but she'd told me not to. "See you tomorrow. Unless I just happen to get sick."

She giggled and said, "You thinking about being sick?"

"I'd love to, but I don't think my dad would fall for it." He hardly ever let me miss school.

"He's nice, but he's not stupid, huh?"

"Right. Well, see ya."

"See ya."

When I got inside, Gus was sitting at the kitchen table like she might have been waiting for me. "How was school?" she asked.

"*Won*derful," I told her, real sarcastic, and I dumped my books on the table hard. I had lugged home every book because I had to cover them all, and I had assignments in most of them, and altogether I didn't need her of all people asking me how school was right then.

She just looked at me, and then she said, "Well, good," and she got up and went outside.

I watched dumb cartoons for a couple of hours, and then Gus came in and started fixing supper and called me to help her. I sighed and rolled my eyes before I went into the kitchen. Gus asked me to set the table and said, "So how was school, really?"

I just shrugged. Even if she was my real mother or my father I still wouldn't have told her much. What happens at school is for kids to know and adults to wish they could find out. But she stood and stared at me until I had to say something, so I muttered, "Great."

"That bad? What happened?"

"Nothing. I was late to everything and I've got a ton of homework and sixteen books to cover, that's all."

"I can cover the books for you," she said.

I didn't want her doing anything for me, but I didn't want to do it myself either. I didn't know what to say, so I mumbled, "What's for supper?"

"Hamburgs."

"Aw, crud, I had hamburgs for lunch."

Gus's burgers were a lot better than the school's, though. And right after supper Gus went and scrounged around in one of the spare bedrooms and came out with about a dozen rolls of wallpaper.

"This stuff makes great book covers," she said. "Lasts like iron."

"Sounds good to me." That was my dad, doing the dishes and trying to be a ray of sunshine. He had been asking me how school was too, but no way was I going to tell him, or he'd be saying he should have taken me himself.

"Ick," I said. Gus had bad taste in wallpaper. Like, one of the patterns was nothing but black and white piano keys, and another was paisley. But I picked one that wasn't too bad, sort of tie-dye, and Gus went ahead and covered my books for me. There weren't really sixteen. Then she left to go outside again, and I went up to my room and did my homework. There wasn't really all that much. I was done just about the time it started to get dark out.

Just about the time the weird music started up again.

"Oh, for crying out loud." Instead of feeling scared I felt frustrated. I wasn't going to sit there and let that strange noise freak me out, and I didn't feel like chasing after it either. I'd had enough hassle for one day. Without even having to think, I got up, headed out, and went across the street to Rawnie's place.

Somebody I didn't know answered the door, a girl

maybe old enough to drive a car. Slim and pretty. She had to be Rawnie's big sister. "Uh, hi," I said. "Is Rawnie around?"

"Sure. Why don't you go on up and see if she's in her room."

I felt funny going up the stairs in somebody else's house, but that's what I did. The doors were open, and I spotted Rawnie flopped on her bed. Her room was at the front of the house, facing mine, which might work out nice for some kind of fun or trouble sometime. I called, "Hi," and Rawnie looked up and said, "Hey! C'mon in."

I got to her door and I was going to tell her the spook music was floating in the air again or maybe just skip that and make fun of Mr. Kuchwald instead, but as soon as I saw inside her room I forgot everything I was going to say. Because there on her wall was a giant poster of the two hottest guys in the world, and they were Nico Torres and Ty Shaney, with the words NEON SHADOW shining over them.

CHAPTER FOUR

♪

What I thought was the worst day in my life turned into one of the best ones ever.

For starters, Rawnie had the Neon Shadow cassette tape. So the first thing we did after I was done jumping up and down and screaming was we listened to Ty and Nico singing "The Friendship Song."

Hey, I remember when
We were desperadoes
You had a guitar on your back
And I had a gun in my hand
And when it came down to the end
You took the bullet they meant for me
And smiled 'cause you could see
I was gonna be okay
Friend.

Hey, friend, my friend,
You're my father, you're my mother
And my sister and my brother
Neither one of us owns the other

Both of us just stay together
Hey, we're sun and wind
We're yang and yin
We're friends.

Hey, back when we were cops
On them mean streets in Chicago
And somebody sold you out to the Mob
But you knew it wasn't me
I wanted you to run and hide
But you knew you had to stay and fight
And I stood by your side
That's the way we died
Friends. . . .

"That is *so* intense," Rawnie whispered when it was over. She pressed the rewind button to play it again.

I felt the same way. When I listened to that song it was like I wanted something clear down to my bones. But it was hard for me to talk about the way the song started me dreaming. I just said, "Do you think they're really like that?"

"Ty and Nico?"

"Yeah. Do you think that's the way it is for them?"

We were both on Rawnie's bed, which was a big one, and we lay there and looked at the poster, which was almost as big as the bed. Nico and Ty looked back at us as if they could really see us. I looked mostly at Nico. He was the dark one, and when he sang, it was like a black fire burning. People said he was part Cuban, part Navaho Indian, part Greek, and part Korean or something. I didn't care what he was. His face wasn't like anybody else's, and it was so perfect it made me want to cry. There was something secret looking out of his eyes, like he had been hurt bad once and hadn't forgotten. He hardly ever smiled. Ty Shaney had a big, sweet smile, and sky blue eyes, and hair like a lion's blond mane. He was sort of warm and golden all over. I guess he was mostly Irish, but who cared. When he and Nico stood next to each other and sang, they would put their heads together, and their hair would mix, black and blond.

Rawnie reached out and turned the song on again. Then she stared up at the ceiling. When she finally said something, it was quiet, like in church. "I think they're all the way friends, yeah."

"That's what I think too. Like in the song, like they've been together since they were little kids and played games that they were cops and cowboys and stuff." There were kids I'd known since I was little, but none of them were real real friends. I felt like I'd missed out on something already, because once I grew up I could never say I had a best friend I had known since I was in kindergarten.

Rawnie swiveled her head to look at me. "Is that what you think they're talking about? That they grew up together?"

"Well, uh, yeah." Wasn't it?

"I always thought it was more for real. Like they really were desperadoes together once, maybe a hundred years ago."

I just lay there and gawked at her, and Ty and Nico sang, "What we always been is what we're always gonna be. . . ."

"Wow," I whispered. What Rawnie had said hit me almost as deep as the song did.

She sat up. There was something shy about the way she held her head, but something proud too, as if she'd always see things through. Rawnie was never going to be cute like a lot of the girls I knew. She was too beautiful to be cute.

Looking at Ty and Nico instead of at me, she said, "I think it's like the song says, they've always been together. I think they were cops together and really got killed together, like they said. And the lifetime before that they were desperadoes. And before that, maybe soldiers. And before that—"

"Explorers," I said. "Sword fighters."

"Maybe. Or Indian warriors."

"Yeah," I whispered. I could imagine them almost as far back as there were people on earth. They would have been knights who rode to the Crusades together. Musicians helping each other out of tavern brawls. Outlaws rebelling against an evil king. Gladiators who wouldn't fight each other. Charioteers, both of them behind the same team of horses, one driving and one handling the spear. Hunters going out to face a ten-foot bear.

Rawnie said, "When they were Indian warriors, I think it would have been, like, Nico got captured and tortured by the enemy Indians, but Ty rescued him."

I knew just what she meant. Nico had that look

about him, as if there were scars on his back. But he wasn't like a victim, more like a survivor. I said, "Don't you think probably Nico rescued Ty sometimes too?"

"Yeah. Probably a lot."

"Probably they saved each other hundreds of times."

"Not just each other."

"No. Other people too. They would have always been, you know, heroes."

The tape went on to the next song, which was about true love, and I sighed and said, "I wish I was a boy."

Just knowing Rawnie loved Neon Shadow too, and talking about Ty and Nico with her the way we had been doing, had turned the whole rotten day around. But now she looked surprised, and she said, "You'd want to be a boy? What for? Boys are jerks."

"Not—I don't mean like the creeps in school." Not like Brent Pimpleface and the other buttheads. There was so much difference between the boys I was used to seeing and the kind of boy I was talking about that they might as well be different species. "I mean—I mean like Nico and Ty."

It seemed to me that boys had some special sort of magic for being with each other. Even the obnoxious boys I knew—the heads or the jocks or the bikers or the skaters on the parking lots together—stuck with each other, it seemed to me, like nobody would ever stick with me. They did dangerous things together, and helped each other out. They were strong. Some of them were sports stars.

Rawnie didn't quite seem to understand. All she did was look at Ty and Nico and sigh and say, "They're hot, all right."

I burst out, "It just seems to me like girls don't do anything."

"Except their hair." Now she was getting it.

"And Nair."

"And hassle each other."

"Over boys."

"Who are jerks, like I told you before."

"Except for Nico and Ty."

"Well, yeah." Rawnie lay back against her pillow again. "Which one do you like best?"

"Nico. I mean, I like them both, but I—Nico—"

"I get the idea." She grinned at me. It was a world-class grin, though she didn't seem to use it very often. "I like them both, but I, uh, *really* like Ty. At least we don't have to fight over which one we like."

"As if either of us is ever going to get near either of them."

"Hey, we'll be within a mile of them when they come to the Arena week after next."

"What?" I sat straight up. "They're coming *here?*"

"Didn't you know that?"

"No! Oh, my God!" Out where I went to school before, nobody knew anything. I hopped off the bed and jumped up and down on the floor. "Oh, my God, we *gotta* see them, we gotta get tickets!"

"In your *dreams,* Harper! I tried. Tickets were sold out months ago."

It was happening again. This day reeked. I opened my mouth and wailed like a baby.

"But you better believe I'm gonna be there outside the Arena to see them go in," Rawnie said.

"I'll be with you."

Before I went home she lent me the Neon Shadow tape and the Neon Shadow issue of *Spin* too. So it was still a super day after all. Then she walked down to the front door with me.

"So I'll see you tomorrow morning. Hey, at least you'll have books to carry in front of your chest this time."

I didn't give that comment the sort of smart-mouth retort it deserved, because I wasn't listening to her, I heard something strange and familiar. She had the door open, both of us were out on the stoop, and way off in the darkness it was happening again. Off behind Gus's big house, it might have been just beyond the creek or six miles behind, but somewhere out there, dim lavender lights were floating and flickering. And there was the distant, heartachy sound of what was maybe a guitar, but maybe not. And maybe more than one. But who could tell?

I said to Rawnie, "Do you see it? Do you hear it?"

"Yes."

I told her between my teeth, "I am *going* to find out what is going on."

"Okay. Me too. Now?"

She was willing to come with me again? But it had been too long a day already. Also, I'd been thinking. "No, not now. Let me do my research first."

"Huh?"

"Gus."

"Yeah," she said real soft, and she came down the

CHAPTER
FIVE

♪

As it turned out, school went a little better the rest of the week. I carried my books hugged to my chest the way Rawnie said, and the girls all liked the wallpaper covers, and the boys gave me some trouble all right, but not the kind I was dreading. So I stayed out of Mr. Kuchwald's office.

I met some girls I liked, especially an eighth-grade girl named Alabaster Bowman, who was really cool. I guess some of the boys were okay too, if you said it quick. Even some of the heads. Like Benjy Jacobs, the boy who got lost in Gus's yard once. He had real long hair and a skull painted on his jacket and a safety pin in his ear, but he was okay to talk to as long as he wasn't with his friends. Rawnie and I walked home from school with him on Friday, and he seemed pretty nice.

"Hey, dudette," he said to me. "I heard about you." Which didn't sound nice at first, but what he meant was that he'd heard I lived with Gus.

"I wouldn't go near that place again if you gave me the winning lottery ticket," he said.

"Yeah," I told him. "I heard about you too."

"I bet you did. Listen, I still feel like people are playing a joke on me. I couldn't have been lost in there for two days. It only felt like a few hours."

"At nighttime?"

"Sure, it was night. I mean, I went in there to see what I could liberate. You don't do that in the daytime."

"Did you hear anything?"

"Huh? No. Nothing special."

"See anything?"

"Huh?"

Rawnie had caught on and started helping me out with her own questions. "Did you see, like, colored lights?"

"I wish there would have been a light! I couldn't see a damn thing. That's why I couldn't find my way out."

"Could you find your way *in?*" Rawnie asked.

"Huh?"

I tried. "How far did you get?"

"Not very. I was stuck the whole time like in a damn maze, if you know what I mean."

I knew exactly what he meant.

"Do me a favor," he told us when we got to his house. "Don't say hi to Spooky McCogg for me. I want her to forget I ever lived."

"Sure," I said.

"Okay," Rawnie said. "Bye, Benjy."

She and I walked on to the next block, where we lived, and then she told me, "Don't always expect Benjy to talk with you like a real person. When he's around here he's okay, but when he's with the other heads he's a jerk just like the rest of them."

"Why do boys do that?"

"I don't know. They just do."

"Girls sort of do that too," I said. "Especially once they get in high school."

"Tell me! Me'n my sister used to be real close. But now she'll just turn against a person. If there's a boy she wants, she'll turn against her best friend to get him."

I was curious. "Does she usually get the boy she wants?"

"Yeah. If you can believe her. Harper, that makes me think. How did your dad and Spooky McCogg get together? Did she go after him?"

"Sorta looks that way, doesn't it?" I complained.

"C'mon!" Rawnie did a little dance. "Tell me how she did it."

"How should I know? He took this found-objects art class she was teaching, and next thing I noticed they were practically married already."

"You don't like her much, do you?"

"Well . . ." A week before I would have said no duh, I didn't like Gus a bit. But now I wasn't sure.

The thing was, as I had told Rawnie, I had research to do. I was starting to spend time with Gus, trying to figure out what was going on in her head and her backyard. I had been helping her with stuff after school, talking with her after supper, kind of spying on her. And the more time I spent around her, the more I got interested in her and all her junk. If being interested in a person is the same thing as liking her, then I had kind of sort of started to like Gus.

I had been telling Rawnie that the junk Gus had in the yard was nothing compared with the stuff she had in some of the sheds. They used to be for cows or something, but now they were full of things like a calliope from a circus, and elk antlers, and a cadaver bag with a broken zipper, and big old wooden radios, and big old jukeboxes full of colored glass tubes.

"She's kind of fun," I told Rawnie. "Come on over tonight and you'll see what I mean."

So she did. As soon as she got in the front door she stood and stared at the hanging sofa, the plow-blade ship in a bottle, the fancy tin ceiling, and all the rest of it. "Radical!" she exclaimed.

"Haven't you ever been in here before?"

"No! How would I?"

"Come on in," my father called from the kitchen. "Would you like some pizza, Rawnie?"

She had eaten her supper, but a person can always fit in a slice of pizza. It was good, and she said so.

"Don't tell me, tell Gus." Dad looked smug as a cat. I'd never seen him as mellow as he was these days. He hardly ever growled at me even when I growled at him.

Gus called over, "I bought it at Safeway all by myself." She was working on one of her art projects. The kitchen was sort of half her studio. It was a big room with skylights and a huge table, and we ate at one end and she messed with her junk on the other end. Right now she was mounting weird stuff on an old board like from barn siding. She had a beat-up eagle from the top of a flagpole on there, and a smashed Pepsi can, and an old license plate, Texas 231959. "What else do you think I should put on, Groover and company?" she said to Rawnie and me. "Tell you what. Let's do this one by committee. Why don't we go scrounge around and see if we can find something?"

"*Ex*cellent," Rawnie said.

So next thing we were all down in the basement poking around, Dad too, poking in boxes and saying, "What's this?" one after the other to Gus.

"What's this?" I had found a metal thing shaped sort of like a seashell.

"Squirrel cage blower."

"Huh?" Who would blow on a squirrel in a cage?

"It blows air. That other one's a biscuit blower. Don't ask me."

"What's this?" Dad held up a circle of glass something like a bike reflector, only white.

"Bott's dot. They used to put them in along the line in roads."

"What's this?" I had a sort of wooden pyramid with a metal pointer.

"Metronome."

"Ew! What are these?" Rawnie held up a handful of pinkish things like marbles, only they weren't marbles.

"Rubber eyeballs."

"Ew, sick! What are they for?"

"Biology class, I guess. I dunno. Ammunition? You girls want them for school?"

We looked at each other and started to smile, but

Dad said, "No. Gus, behave. You'll get them in trouble."

"Hey!" I had found a box full of wide silvery tape.

"Duck tape."

"*Huh?*"

"You've heard about people getting their ducks in a row? That's how they keep them that way, with duck tape."

Dad said, "It's *duct* tape. Don't pay any attention to her, Skiddo. She'll lead you astray." The way he was grinning said the opposite.

Gus turned away and snapped on the radio. She was always doing that. She would go for maybe about three minutes talking with you, and then her eyes would sort of fog over and she had to have her music. There was a radio in every shed and just about every room of the house, and they were all tuned to—not oldies, exactly, but something a little bit better. She called it classic rock. It always had a cookin' beat, and this time was no different. Rawnie heard it for about one second and started to dance.

"You like my music?" Gus said.

"Yeah, but I like Neon Shadow better!"

"You too?"

Gus and Dad knew how I felt about Neon Shadow. Gus said that back when she was a kid, girls screamed over the Beatles. Before that it was Elvis. I didn't see what was so great about any of them.

"I hear Neon Shadow is coming to the Arena next week," Gus said.

It didn't take Rawnie and me long to make it clear to Gus and Dad what we thought of the fact that Neon

Shadow was going to be practically in our front yard
and we didn't have tickets. Between the two of us I
guess we made a lot of noise. In fact I remember
going, "*Waaaah!*" like a baby, which made Gus blink
several times rapidly, looking half-worried and half-
laughing, the way she did a lot of the time.

"Well," she said, "listen. I have a friend who has a
friend who has a friend. Howsabout if I try to get some
tickets."

Now Rawnie and I were jumping up and down and
screaming. Dad sighed and rolled his eyes.

"Hey, I can't promise," Gus said. "But I'll try."

It took us awhile to get back to scrounging. Then
Dad found a bone wrench and a moon wrench, some
lamp parts, and a broach, whatever a broach is, but
nothing Gus wanted to use. She led the scrounging
expedition out to the sheds, where Rawnie saw the
calliope and a ton of other stuff besides. There was an
electric violin, which was really just a plug-in board
with strings. There were old record players, a stove
shaped like a Chinese dragon, a tin whistle, an eyecup,
and a Dobro. There were boxes of grommets and gas-
kets and car parts and the glass reflector plugs from
old telephone poles and flutophones.

"I give up," Gus said, meaning she didn't know
what to put on her folk art. "I'm just going to have to
think about it."

"Hey, Gus, what is this?" I said. It was a thing sort
of like a miniature piano, but it had some kind of
machine instead of a piano back.

"That's a Mellotron. You know how you hear violins in the songs on the radio? Most of the time they're

not really violins. Nowadays they're usually synthe-sized, but it used to be they used a Mellotron."

"Huh?"

"Huh, my eye. The back houses a bunch of tape loops of violins sounding different notes. You press the keys, the violins play."

"Huh!"

Rawnie was looking across the yard, which wasn't easy to do, considering how much stuff was in the way. "What's in that little shed with the big hex sign?" she wanted to know.

"The pigeon coop? Dead axes, mostly."

"Dead axes?"

But Gus wasn't listening. She had folk art on her mind like a bug in her ear, and she was heading back toward the house. Dad went to stick a load of wash in the machine, and Rawnie and I went up to my room so she could see what it looked like, and by the time Rawnie was ready to go home, Gus had disappeared somewhere again.

"Tell your—tell her thanks for the pizza and every-thing," Rawnie said to me. I watched her go across the street. She never walked anywhere, and she didn't exactly run either. This time she was doing the Loco-motion.

Tell Gus thanks for the pizza and everything. "And everything" meant trying to get tickets for the Neon Shadow concert. It wasn't going to be easy, because she had to get three or four. Neon Shadow was a clean group, no drugs in the parking lot or anything like that, but it was still a rock concert and it would still be wild, not something Rawnie and I could go to by ourselves. I knew my dad—he would never let it happen. We would have to have at least one parent with us, and if Gus could get enough tickets for that many people, it would be almost a miracle.

Tell her thanks? I hadn't thanked her myself, and I should have. I should be nicer to her. She was nice to me. And it wasn't her fault if she was built like a truck or fell in love with my dad.

Right that minute before I lost my nerve I went looking for her.

It was getting dark and the weird guitar music was due to start, but I didn't care. I just wanted to find Gus and be nice to her for a minute or two before I forgot and started wise-mouthing her again. She was out in the backyard probably, so that was where I went. I checked each shed. Nothing. The farthest one from the house was the pigeon coop with its big hex sign, which wasn't a regular star hex but a sort of swirl pattern in all colors. The hex faced the yard, which was odd. Most people liked hexes to face the road so people could see them. But there was nothing on the street side of the pigeon coop except the door.

Anyway, I went there last and looked inside. Nothing except a bunch of old electric guitars, bent up and stripped down until they were nearly skeletons.

Dead axes?

Then I blinked hard, because one by one they were floating up off the shadowy floor, and fading like ghosts, and—

Disappearing into the wall. Right in front of me. It was totally gonzo, yet I stood there and watched and felt like it all made sense, like I knew what was happening. Dead axes, and they were not disappearing, exactly, they were going through a sort of twilight door to another place. Another dimension.

On the far side of the hex-sign wall I heard the music starting.

It was just a clicking, like a drummer setting a rhythm with his sticks, and a strumming, like a guitarist tuning. Concert night, and I was backstage. Wow, there was no time to be afraid. I had to see what was going on, and by then I felt sure that I wouldn't need to go any farther than the other side of the pigeon coop.

I went outside to look, and I was right.

The lights were on, all colors like the hex sign. Somebody was setting up the drum kit. I could tell because washtubs and buckets and old hubcaps and things were lifting off the ground and floating through the air to where the drum riser was, the plywood platform on top of the big red Caddy, and then they'd disappear. Actually they were fading and disappearing the whole time, as they moved. But I could see them. The world was getting dark, but the lights blazed brighter all the time and it seemed as if I could see more every minute. I could see a Mellotron settle down and turn into a concert keyboard. I could see bare-bone guitars flying out of the hex sign, coming right through it, coming out to play. The music in the air was louder than I'd ever heard it, and since I'd forgotten to be scared of it, I was dancing where I stood, my feet going like Rawnie's always did, before I realized how much I liked it. What a rhythm! I could hear the drums, the axes, the deep notes on the key-

board. And voices. For the first time I could hear
voices singing, dark and hot.

People. The band. Who were they?

I could just barely see them. They were like cloud
wisps in the air. But I could hear them, and I could see
their instruments a little, and I could tell what they
were doing. They were playing lead guitar and bass
and organ and drums and tambourine and sax, they
were filling in with vocals, they were making music.
And it was some of the best music I'd ever heard.
Almost as good as Neon Shadow, though I couldn't
quite make out the words.

My feet still wanted to dance, but my brain took
over and started sputtering, and I stood there with my
mouth open. Then all the music stopped at once, and
the people—had there been people? Now I couldn't
see a thing. Just old metal pails and upside-down washtubs and a hubcap or two on top of the convertible's
plywood cover where I thought there had been
drums.

And Gus standing beside me with a big old twelve-
string guitar hanging by a braided strap from her neck.

She was looking curiously at me. Then she
strummed the twelve-string a little, and I could tell
right away she really knew how to play it. She made
that big old guitar sound like a roomful of rockers
jamming. For half an instant I wondered if she had
been the one making the twilight music all along. And
I knew that was what she wanted me to think. But it
wasn't like she was trying to fool me, really. It was
more like she was offering me a chance to back away,

to tell myself, Okay, I just heard Gus messing around on her guitar.

Forget that. I knew what I had seen, what I had heard. There had been a band. A hot hot hot happenin' band.

"I heard them," I said to Gus, kind of loud—I had forgotten all about thanking her or being nice to her. "I saw them. They were *good.* Who are they?"

She just stood and looked at me with her fog gray eyes wide open. When she got her mouth under control and said something, it wasn't exactly an answer.

"Groover," she declared, "you are something else. Girl, you sure must love rock music."

CHAPTER
SIX
♪

"Gus is going to teach me how to play guitar," I told Rawnie next time I saw her, which was Saturday afternoon.

"She plays guitar?"

"Yeah." I hesitated. "I think it's sort of been her we've been hearing."

"Sort of?"

"Well, yeah. Sort of. I dunno."

I didn't mean to lie to Rawnie. But Gus never had really given me an answer about what I had seen and heard. And it had been so beautiful, the music and the feeling around the music, that I had dreamed neon rainbow dreams all night, and I didn't know how to describe to anybody what had happened. I wasn't afraid of what was in Gus's backyard anymore, and that made me feel lonesome. Different, as if I had put myself on the wrong side of a wall from everybody else. Apart from other people, the ones I couldn't tell. Well, how was I supposed to explain something I didn't understand myself? But maybe that was why—

feeling strange, I mean—maybe that was why I acted
so dumb in school on Monday and let Rawnie down.

It started when Aly Bowman asked me to sit with
her at lunch. Rawnie always saved me a seat at lunchtime, and the kids at our table were lots of fun. But
there was something about Alabaster. I guess she
wasn't pretty, because she had kind of a beak of a
nose, but she was so cool. She acted like she didn't
care about parents or teachers or what they thought
of her, and I kinda wished I could be that way. I liked
the cool way she dressed too. She was real thin, and
she had her hair dyed bright blond and cut real real
short, only about an inch long, except she'd left a
forelock of long spiral-perm bangs in front. She always
wore black, like a black bomber jacket and a black
leather skirt. She even had her fingernails painted
black. And she had one ear pierced in three places.
Altogether she seemed a lot more sure of herself than
any kid I ever knew, and she was a couple years older
than me too. So I was excited that she wanted to be
friends with me, and I sat with her.

The girls at her table were okay. We played a game
called MASH, which stands for Mansion, Apartment,
Shack, House. It's a kind of fortune-telling game about
who you're going to marry, what sort of place you're
going to live in, and whether you're going to be di-
vorced. And how many kids you're going to have, and
where, like in the bathroom sink or what, and whether
they're boys or girls, and whether they're black or
white. That last thing seemed dumb to me, but the
girls giggled over it a lot. They made me put Brent, the

one who had pinched me, on my MASH as one of the boys I might marry, but he got crossed out right away, thank God.

Rawnie was kind of quiet when we walked home together and to school together the next morning. So when Aly asked me to sit with her at lunch, I said, "I'm going to sit with Rawnie today. I think she's mad."

"That's dumb." Then Aly giggled. "But I guess she would be dumb, wouldn't she?"

I didn't know what that meant and I didn't want to ask and look stupid. Thing is, I should have stood up for Rawnie right then, but I didn't. I just said, "I'm going to sit with her today anyway."

"No, you're not. You sit with me all the time or you don't sit with me at all."

I had been figuring I could sit with Aly one day, Rawnie the next. And I didn't like what Aly had just said. It didn't seem fair. But then again, I sort of did like it because not being fair was part of the way she was cool.

Anyway, I thought, I got to see Rawnie before school and after school and on Saturdays, wasn't that enough? I only got to see Aly in school. So I sat with her and her gang again.

We had a lot of fun. Those girls didn't care what they said. They mocked everything and everybody and made me laugh and laugh. When it was time to go back to class Aly said to me, "See, wasn't that better than sitting with a certain little jig?"

I just stood there with my mouth open while she walked away. I mean, of course I knew Rawnie was black, but it had just never occurred to me that it should make any difference. I don't usually think about people that way, like being Jewish or Italian or Vietnamese or Puerto Rican or whatever is all that important, except that it's nice to know where you come from. Or at least I never used to think about it much until I came to this school. But that afternoon I kept thinking about the differences between people and I started to wonder if maybe I was missing something. Having attitude about other people seemed to be part of being cool. Aly always had a name for everybody, like "He's a zipperhead" or "She's a crotch watcher," or whatever.

On the way home Rawnie was real quiet again, but I was still thinking so much about what Aly had said that I blurted out, "Are you all the way black?" I mean, it wasn't real obvious. Calling her black made about as much sense as calling Nico Torres Korean, or calling me French because my one grandmother came from France.

Rawnie looked at me and her mouth was pressed into a flat thin line. She said, "Does it matter?"

"No, not really. I just—"

"You don't want to be friends with me because I'm black, is that it, Harper Ferree? You'd rather hang around with the skinheads? Well, forget it. Forget everything. You can just walk by yourself from now on."

She took off running, and she really knew how to do that. I couldn't have caught up with her even if I'd tried, which I didn't, because she'd just made me really mad. What did she think I was, some sort of baby? I could choose who I hung around with, and I could take care of myself. I yelled after her, "I don't need you to walk with me!"

I really didn't. I walked to school and back by myself the next three days, and I wasn't afraid of the street corner guys, even when they hollered at me. I was too angry and miserable to feel afraid.

Rawnie and I weren't speaking. If we met each other in the hall at school, we looked past each other. I hadn't gone over to her house and she hadn't come over to mine. At lunch on Wednesday I sat with Aly and her friends and made it a point to laugh hard so Rawnie would hear me. By Thursday I wasn't laughing at all.

"What's the matter with you?" Aly wanted to know. She didn't ask it like she cared—more like she wanted me to get out of her face. But I told her anyway. I needed to talk to somebody, and she was the only friend I had now.

"Rawnie's the matter," I said. "She makes me mad." What I really meant was that I felt awful that she was mad at me.

"So, who cares about her? You just stick with us white girls, babe. We're better."

I wish I could say I got up and told her off, but I didn't. I just sat there and felt like my brain wanted to scream. If I went against Aly, I wouldn't have any friends left at all. But Aly didn't seem so cool anymore.

Really Aly wasn't my only friend, there was one more. Only she wasn't anywhere near my age, so I hadn't thought of her right away. It was Gus. All the time I wasn't going to Rawnie's house she'd been teaching me to play guitar, and she was so funny and nice I wondered why I hadn't liked her before. We didn't go out in the backyard to play though. We didn't go anywhere near where the red Cadillac convertible was. We just sat in the house.

That night we tried to get my stupid fingers to do a G chord, but they wouldn't stretch. Nothing was going right. I said to her, "Gus, what's a skinhead?"

She gave me a worried look. "Well, it depends," she said. "There's skinheads and there's skinheads. Which kind do you mean?"

"Whatever kind we've got around here."

Gus sighed, not like she was annoyed but like she was sad. She said, "Around here we've got the Nazi kind."

"What's that?"

"White supremacists. People who say all other people are inferior to white people. People who are bigoted against most of the world and want to take it over, the way Hitler wanted to take over."

I was starting to understand now. I had seen Aly's boyfriend, with his shaved head and combat boots.

"Oh, jeez," I said.

"They stand for violence. Lately they've been marching with the Ku Klux Klan."

"Oh, jeez." I felt sick.

"You been having problems with skinheads? They been giving you trouble because you're friends with Rawnie?"

I guess she hadn't noticed. I mumbled, "I'm not friends with Rawnie anymore."

"No?"

I shook my head, looking down at the guitar Gus had given me. It was a nice little electric guitar, bright enamel red, like the Caddy out back.

"You sure? Just because you're fighting right now doesn't mean you can't still be friends."

"I think I blew it pretty bad."

"Ouch." Dad would have been trying to get all the details out of me, but Gus could tell I didn't want to talk about it. I guess it made it easier that I was not her own kid. She was pretty good about leaving things up to me. Which is what she did next. She said, "Bummer, Groover. And here's another one. I got the Neon Shadow tickets all right, but they would only give me two."

My brain felt tired, and I hadn't been thinking much about the Neon Shadow concert anyway. I just looked at her.

She said, "That band is really hot. I couldn't get more for love or money."

"Um, two is okay. Thanks, Gus."

"You don't have to thank me." It was the first time I'd thanked her for anything, and now she sounded like Rawnie, not wanting to be thanked. Jeez, I missed Rawnie.

Gus said, "You just have to figure out what to do with them." She stood up and got the tickets out of a cigar jar and handed them to me. They were electric red, and they were in a little envelope with NEON SHADOW in neon gold letters against a shadow blue background. I wondered how much she'd paid for them, but I didn't really want to know, so I didn't ask.

The concert was Saturday. All day Friday I tried to cheer myself up by thinking about going to it with my dad or Gus, whichever one wanted to take me. But it didn't work. I kept on thinking about Rawnie.

She wasn't saving me a seat at lunchtime anymore, of course, and I didn't want to sit with Aly and her snooty gang, so I went off to the back of the cafeteria and sat by myself. There were other people I could have sat with, I guess. Really, there were more nice people in that school than not, once you got past the clothes and haircuts and stuff. But I just didn't feel like talking to anybody. Same between classes. And same walking home. I could have caught up with Benjy and his sister and walked with them. But I didn't.

That night at supper I asked Gus, "Do you mind if I just give the concert tickets to Rawnie?"

"Fine with me."

My dad looked real surprised. "Harper, what are you talking about? Gus got those tickets for you."

"I know."

"So don't you think you'd better use them? Do you have any idea how much trouble and expense—"

"Buddy," Gus interrupted him in a real quiet way, "Groover knows what she's doing, and I think I do too." She nodded at me. "Go ahead, Groover, run those tickets over to Rawnie if you're done eating."

I looked at my dad, and he looked kind of bug-eyed for a minute like he might explode, but then he nodded. "Gus says it's okay. But you aren't really finished with your supper, are you?"

"Um, yeah, can I be excused? I'm not hungry."

"Just take the tickets," I told Rawnie.

"I can't! Anyhow, Dad would never let me. They must be worth a couple hundred dollars."

"Gus said you could have them."

"But I don't feel right—"

"Listen, I'm not going without you, so you might as well take them."

We went back and forth like that awhile, and I guess we might have kept going like that until Saturday except that I thought I heard something. I stopped arguing with Rawnie and said, "C'mon!" to her instead, and took her by the hand and hustled her down the stairs.

"Huh?" she kept saying. "Harper!"

But once I got her outside she understood. The notes came drifting on the air not much louder than dandelion seed, but we both knew what they were. We stood still, listening hard. Rawnie whispered, "They're playing 'The Friendship Song.'"

A car came along, and we couldn't hear the music over the swish it made, that's how faint it was. I said, "Come on," and I led her across the street. "This way." We weren't going to go through the maze. I took her around back of the sheds. Once I looked at her to see how she was doing, because she was so quiet. But she didn't seem scared. Just nervous. A little. I guess she could see I wasn't scared anymore.

We could hear voices, deep distant echoing voices that did not belong to Nico and Ty, singing "The Friendship Song." The music was kind of like a big radio turned way down low, but we could tell it was right on the other side of the sheds. We got to the pigeon coop, and I started around the corner. "Harper," Rawnie whispered behind me, "I can't go out there!"

"Yes, you can." I turned back and took her hand again, but I didn't drag her. She walked out by herself.

So there we were, Rawnie and me, standing in the open, side by side, and there was Gus sitting on the bumper of her big red Caddy. She had her guitar in her arms like a baby but she wasn't playing it right then. She was just smiling at us fit to split. We couldn't see anything else except now and then flashes of colored light amid something like mist in the air. But all the time the music went on.

> *. . . what we've always been*
> *Is what we're always gonna be.*
> *We're yang and yin,*
> *We're sun and wind,*
> *We're eternity. . . .*

"Right on, Groover and company!" Gus called to us. "Me'n the band been rooting for you two."

CHAPTER
SEVEN

♪

Saturday came, and what should have been one of the happiest nights in my life turned into one of the saddest and scariest.

Rawnie and I were *both* going to the Neon Shadow concert, that's why it should have been happy. After she went home Friday night Rawnie talked to her father, and Saturday morning Mr. Stellow called the Arena and found out there was a soundproof waiting room for parents. So parents could take their kids and be right there in case their kids needed them, yet not have to pay for tickets. Mr. Stellow offered to take us, and he came over and talked with my dad about it, and I don't know what he said, but somehow he made Dad say okay. Or maybe it wasn't Mr. Stellow at all, maybe it was Gus. Or the puppy dog look I was wearing. Or maybe my dad was just starting to loosen up finally. Anyway, he said I could go with Rawnie.

Before we went to the Arena, though, we went to Just Jewelry at the shopping mall and got each other friendship necklaces. They were metal chains with metal pendants, not fake gold or fake anything, just real metal. The pendants were shaped sort of like fish, Rawnie's with the head up and mine with the head down. Rawnie's said BE and FRI, and mine said, ST and ENDS. The pendants fit together like a circle, and together they said BEST FRIENDS. We put them on right there in the store.

"I'm going to wear mine all the time," Rawnie said.

"Me too," I told her. "Even when I'm asleep."

"Until you're a hundred?"

"Yep. Or dead."

So it really was an awesome day—so far. And then we ate at Wendy's. Mr. Stellow treated us. And then he got us to the Arena early and waited with us while we waited for Neon Shadow's limousine to pull in. When it finally came, there was such a crowd that we couldn't see a thing, but we didn't really care, because we were going to the concert.

Mr. Stellow helped us get to our seats. "You two stick together and don't go *anywhere* else," he told us once we were there, like we couldn't find our way around. Like, what if we had to go to the bathroom? But we said we would, and he went to the parents' room to wait.

It was so rad. Rawnie and I had way front good seats. "How did Spooky . . . How did Gus do it?" Rawnie yelled in my ear. It was loud in there already, so a person had to yell.

"I dunno. Spook power?"

"Don't *say* that."

The opening band came on, and people whistled and clapped, but nobody screamed yet. These guys were okay, they had some good songs, but I think they

were lip-synching or something. When they sang or
when they moved around or jumped up or went down
on their knees, it was like they were just going through
motions. I don't even remember what they looked like
or their band's name. They were not Neon Shadow.

When they went off and we sat waiting in the loud
crowd, Rawnie yelled to me, "I can't stand it! I'd faint
right now, except I'd miss everything!"

"I'm going to cry, and I look like a sick duck when
I cry!"

Everything went black. We grabbed each other's
hands. People started screaming, and so did we. And
then the spotlight came on, and there they were, and
everybody jumped up and stood on top of their seats,
including us. And it was Nico, Nico and Ty, only about
twenty feet away from Rawnie and me, and the music
was all around us, the drummer pounding out a beat
like a million hearts and the guitars carrying it up, up,
crying out loud, like me, and Ty and Nico were singing.

"Life is sharp as a knife," Rawnie sang along with
them. "I know we won't grow old, but I don't see how
we can ever die." It was a song called "Scars." We
knew all their songs, but I couldn't sing, I was all
choked up. There they were, Nico and Ty, right there,
breathing the same air with me; if I reached out hard
enough maybe I could touch them. . . . When they
sang, it was like a prayer, they meant it. They lived the
music, they let it move them around, they surren-
dered to it even when it slammed them to their knees.

"Oh," I whispered. "Oh." Nico had real tears in his
eyes. One crept out and shone on his face. On me it

would be just a crybaby tear, but on him it looked like a jewel.

"Did they look at us?" Rawnie yelled in my ear. "Did they see us?"

"Maybe."

"Oh, my God, you really think so? I'd die just to say hi to them."

I didn't want to say hi to them—I wanted to *be* them. To be in a band, me and my buddies against the world, to be a beautiful rock outlaw playing hero guitar with a very all-time best friend by my side—it seemed like all I could ever want. And everything I knew I could never have.

Lights were flashing, the guitars turned tornado colors, and the keyboards thundered. Neon Shadow swung into "Dark Ride," which was about dying, but I didn't care if I died someday. I did what Nico and Ty did, I let myself give in, I let tornado guitars and thunder drums take me deep, deeper into themselves, farther than I had ever gone before into a place where everything was made of raw voice and bent metal and hard rock music.

And I was still standing on my chair, I was still stretching my hands into the air and yelling along with the song and crying, but something had changed. I could see better than ever before. I could see more than ever before. And I saw something big as Neon Shadow coiled under the roof of the stage, something waiting just above the lights, something dark. At first it seemed like a dark fog, a black smoke thing, a hanging cloud. But I kept looking at it, because it was right over Ty and Nico and because I wanted to be like them, I wanted to be a desperado, a hero, not a middle-school girl with her books over her chest. Not scared. And as I looked I could see it more clearly.

"Rawnie," I whispered. There was no way she could have heard me, but I felt her hand clutch at mine. She had let the music take her deep into the same place. She saw it too.

It was—huge, bigger than any python or anaconda, but it was made of air and darkness, and it had wings, scaly ones, webbed like bat wings, right behind its blunt coffin-shaped head. It was a snake, or a black angel, or something I didn't have a name for. And it was on the move. It slithered. I saw its tongue flicker like lightning. Its head swung down.

"Maybe it's just part of the show?" Rawnie begged me.

It wasn't. We both knew it wasn't. But there were people packed all around us so we couldn't move. There was nothing we could do.

It's midnight and the flowers are buried
Time to take the long ride,
Time to take the dark ride.

Ty and Nico sang like a high wind, they had not glanced up, they did not see the huge death hanging right above them, but Nico looked pale and sick. The music did not move him around now. He stood by himself and swayed on his feet, and he was supposed to be at the other mike with Ty, I could see that by the way Ty was staring at him.

The six-foot black-coffin head reached for Nico. "No!" I screamed, and I hid behind my hands.

Rawnie told me afterward that it didn't bite him or even touch him. It just breathed on him, and he closed his eyes and fell flat on the stage. And the music stopped. The yelling and screaming stopped, and everything got very quiet except for people asking each other what was happening.

When I looked again, I didn't see any snake, any shadow or fog, nothing except Nico lying there.

Ty reached him first, and kneeled by him, and felt his neck and chest, and yelled, "Somebody call an ambulance!" Then I heard people crying, and they weren't even me.

It seemed to take forever for the ambulance to come. Police came in and cleared most of the people out of the Arena, including us, and then Rawnie's father didn't know where to find us, and it was a mess. We just stood against a wall and hung on to each other. We couldn't talk or anything. Mr. Stellow put his arms around both of us when he finally tracked us down, and he walked us to the car that way. He didn't want us to see the ambulance go.

"I'm sorry," he kept saying as if it was his fault if Nico died. Which of course it wasn't, it wasn't anybody's fault. Unless . . .

"Do you think Gus sent that snake thing?" Rawnie whispered to me in the back of the car.

"Don't," I said. It made me feel cold, what she'd said. Why would Gus do a thing like that? But I knew what Rawnie meant. The snake had looked like it might have something to do with Gus. It was made of air and shadows, like the band that played in her back-yard at dusk.

I felt so bad that I didn't even want to talk to Gus when I got home. She and Dad were surprised to see me home so early and they wanted to know what had happened, but I wouldn't tell them. I couldn't talk about it. They could see I was really upset, so Dad called Rawnie's place to find out what was going on while Gus helped me get to bed. After she left I just lay there with my eyes wide burning open in the dark, staring at those big heavy metal circles that swung in the windows. A little later Dad and Gus came to my door.

"It's serious," Dad said, "but Nico's made it so far. He's in the intensive care unit."

Mr. Stellow was a prosthetic technician, so he knew a lot of the people at the hospital, and he had been able to find out what was wrong. Nico was un-conscious because of some kind of rare syndrome. His blood cells were breaking apart, but there was noth-ing the hospital could do for him except try to keep him alive with transfusions and oxygen.

"Bad scene, Groover," Gus said to me. "Anything I can do for you? Talk to me."

But I didn't want to. Even though I was under three blankets, I still felt too cold to tell her what was really bothering me. Her or Dad or anybody else. Only Rawnie knew about what she and I had seen.

I made it through the night somehow. And the next day, Sunday, I watched TV and listened to the radio just about all day to hear the news broadcasts.

Every one said something about Nico. He had collapsed onstage in front of fifteen thousand people. There was a crowd of well-wishers in front of the hospital. Mounted police had been called in to keep control. The rock music world was in a state of shock. Nico remained in critical condition, with Ty at his bedside.

Around the middle of the afternoon my dad ordered me into the kitchen and made me eat something. And when I got back to the TV, they were saying that Ty Shaney had left the city. He and the rest of the band members were continuing the Neon Shadow tour.

That didn't make any sense. Ty Shaney was supposed to be like a blood brother to Nico. He shouldn't leave him lying in a hospital alone.

I called Rawnie. It was probably the tenth time that day I'd talked to her, but this time I was so upset I could barely make sense. She said, "Save it, Harper. I'm coming over." Then when she did come over, and I told her what the news had said, she thought I must have heard wrong. She had to see it on the next bulletin before she'd believe me.

"Oh, my God," she said. "Oh, Ty. You traitor. You dirty rat. We thought you were one of the good guys." Her voice sounded like she wanted to cry.

I said, "So now Nico's lying there—"

"I am going to rip up every picture I have of Ty Shaney."

"That won't help Nico. He's all by himself and somebody's got to help him somehow."

My father had come in to hear the news, and we

had forgotten he was there. He was listening to us, and he said, "I bet his folks are there with him."

I said, "I don't think Nico has a mother or a father." I don't know why I knew that. Maybe I'd read it somewhere. Maybe it was just because I knew who he was, the desperado, the dark stranger passing through town, and that kind of person has no family. However I knew, it turned out I was right.

Rawnie and I went outside so we could talk by ourselves, and she said, "Well?"

"Well, what?"

"Well, what are we going to do? We can't let him just lie there and die. It's up to us if we're going to do something."

I looked around as if that could help. Weird junk everywhere. Pipe cactus. Whirligig going round and round. Wind chimes. It would be getting dark soon, and I knew what would happen then.

I said, "I guess we both know who we ought to talk to."

"Yeah. So are we going to go do it now?"

"I guess."

"You ready?"

"I don't know if I'll ever be ready, but we're going to do it anyway."

CHAPTER EIGHT

♪

"Gus," I said, "at the concert, just before Nico fell, there was a, like, a snake hanging over him. A huge snake with scaly wings."

She was out back, still trying to find something that would go with a flagpole eagle, a Texas license plate, and a smashed Pepsi can. When I started she was bent over rooting around so I was talking to her butt, but by the time I was done she was standing bolt straight and facing me. And that was the first time she looked old to me. I mean I always just assumed she was around my dad's age or maybe a little older, but to look at her most of the time she might have been twenty or fifty. She just didn't show an age for sure. But this time she looked kind of gray all over.

She asked Rawnie a question with her eyes, and Rawnie nodded and said, "I saw it too."

"Are you all right? Nightmares?"

"I haven't slept enough to have nightmares yet."

"At least you can joke about it. Groover? You okay?"

"It's not the snake that bothers me, it's worrying about Nico."

"Well, I'm worrying more about you two," Gus said in a soft voice. "You aren't supposed to be able to see the Dark Serpent, either of you."

She knew all about it. "Then you did send it."

"No. No, I don't choose who is to go. I just—provide a place for them." At first I didn't recognize the look on her face, because it was the first time I'd seen her really upset. "For God's sake, Harper, what do you think I am? If I'd known something like that was going to happen at the concert, you girls wouldn't have been there."

We stood staring at each other. Rawnie was the one who said, "What place?"

"Huh?" Gus looked at her.

"Where do they go? Once the Dark Serpent comes for them?"

"These days? Here, mostly."

I felt like there were bugs crawling all over me. I wanted to yell, but all I could do was squeak it out: "All the dead people in the world are in your backyard?"

"No! No, the Dark Serpent only comes for heroes and great lovers and poets." Gus still looked old, but she was starting to get back her pink face and her smile. "The rest of us have to slip out in the more usual way."

I had a feeling she could have told me all the details, and I didn't want to know them. I stood shivering. Rawnie said, "But the ones the Dark Serpent brings—they are here, they make music."

"The ones you are aware of make music. You can't see or hear the others. You two aren't supposed to be able to hear my backyard band either." Gus did not sound sorry that we could, though. In fact she seemed kind of proud. Of us.

I was still hung up on one real basic fact. "Because they're dead," I said. Just trying to make sure.

"Dead, yet not dead." Which didn't help me any. But Gus was not seeing me. She was standing tall and staring far away, and now if I couldn't tell her age, it was because she would never grow all the way old. That scared me a little. When she spoke, it scared me more. She didn't sound like herself. She didn't even sound like a woman. Her voice had gone deep and strange, as if it came out of the center of the earth, as if somebody else was talking through her mouth.

She said: "I am Aengus. I am the master of the afterworlds where heroes dwell. Those who come to me are the ones who will not quite die. I have hosted the feasts at Valhalla, I welcomed King Arthur to Avalon. I was the god of the Blessed Isles, and poets and warriors came to me on horses that ran atop the waves. I was the sunset, and Wyatt Earp rode into my arms. I was on a mountaintop in California, and James Dean and a hundred others came to me there."

I didn't like being scared. It made me mouthy. Too loud, I said, "And now you're *here*?"

"Yes. Why not? All places are under the same holy sky." She looked around at her backyard full of junk, and her eyes were bright as a hawk's. "They lived for metal," she said, "and for the city, and for excess."

I didn't care. "Dead is *dead*," I said. "What's going to happen to Nico?"

"Once he dies, it will depend how long people remember him."

"No!" He couldn't die. I started to cry, and Rawnie put her arms around me, and Gus stooped down to face me.

"I'm sorry," she said, and she had her own voice back, she was just an ordinary person again, a funny-faced woman in a baseball cap. "I'm sorry, I was forgetting what it's like for . . ."

She didn't finish the sentence. I glared at her over Rawnie's shoulder, sniffling. For regular people, she meant. For people who don't have one life after another.

"Harper," she said, real gently this time. "I think he is going to die. He's letting go now. His spirit is already here with the others. It sits and watches and will not sing, but it is here."

It wasn't just that I wanted to help Nico, or save him, or meet him and talk with him. That was partly it, that I felt like Rawnie did, that I would have died to say hi to him and tell him I loved him. But even more it was that I wanted to be something besides what I was, which was an overgrown twelve-year-old girl with not enough guts to tell her father she needed a bra.

We were back at Rawnie's house. She had not ripped up every picture she had of Ty Shaney. It was like we were just too tired. The two of us were flopped on her bed and listening to her radio, numb, waiting for the bad news. We didn't want to eat or talk or anything.

But after a while the want-to-be-something feeling started coming together inside me, and I said to Rawnie, "Listen, if we were—" Then I stopped, because I couldn't say Nico and Ty anymore. They had turned out to be not what we thought they were. Ty anyway. All the Neon Shadow dreams we had made up were lies.

"If we were what?"

"If we were somebody else besides us. If we were heroes, like in a song. What would we do?"

"Just tell me what you're thinking, Harper."

"We'd go get Nico and bring him back."

She turned her head and looked at me in that cat-staring way she had, and after a minute she said, real low, "How?"

"I dunno. How did we get to see the dark snake?"

"It was just—I was all the way into the music."

"Me too. Like I was lost and the whole world was music. Like I was swimming in it."

We looked at each other a minute longer, and then she said in a soft, calm voice, "Go home. Pretend to go to bed. Then sneak out and meet me at the corner of the front porch, where the whirligig is."

I understood. We didn't need to say another word. I just nodded at her and went down her stairs and outside to where the sky was turning silver gray, like a Dobro's belly.

*   *   *

The music started one faint note at a time, coming at us out of the night like it was echoing from someplace very far away. Not so far away in distance, we knew now. We were sitting on the porch, and we just had to go to Gus's backyard. But in another way it was the longest walk anybody could ever take. The Aengus McCogg Backyard Band was performing in a stadium as big as eternity.

"Close your eyes," I whispered to Rawnie. "Listen."

I did the same thing myself and sat and tried to let the music into me. It was hard, because I was afraid. But at the same time it just had to happen, because the music was calling, calling, and it was so beautiful, and I wanted to know what song the band was playing, and I wanted to hear the words.

And slowly, gently, the way dusk turns into dark, it happened, and I could hear the drums clearly, and the quick bell-clustered notes of the guitars, and organ roar, and saxophone wail, and the voices blending and shouting.

> *The angel came and said, Hey, little baby boy*
> *I'm gonna give you a kiss, gonna let you sing*
> *Like a devil in the fire, like a god in the sky.*
> *We said, Daddy don't stop, don't stop,*
> *Don't quit with a taste, we want the whole thing,*
> *Hey, give me your threads, hey, give me those wings*
> *We're gonna dance on the shore while the tide keeps*
>   *coming.*
> *So we took it all, and we bounced it off the*
>   *mountaintop*
> *And every Coke Classic, we drank it to the last drop.*

The angel came and told us, Now say good-bye,
We said, Hey, Daddy, we're not about to die.

I felt somebody touch my hand. I didn't have to look, I knew who it was, but I couldn't exactly remember her name. Or my own. I was me, all right, but also somebody else, somebody more, in this place.

Whatever place this was.

I opened my eyes and looked around at a gray meadow full of strange, steely trees with bare branches. Ahead was the dark path that led toward the concert, toward the stadium, but between me and the path stood a deer with its head up, watching me. It was a tall deer with strong shoulders, a stag, and it had long, pointed metal antlers, the sharpest I had ever seen.

I stood up, and my comrade stood up with me. I looked at her. The smooth tawniness of her face told me nothing, yet everything.

"You don't have a mother either," I said.

"No." She shook her head. "She was in the army, she got killed in an accident. What about yours?"

"She took off right after I was born. I've never even met her. I guess Gus is my mother now."

That name out of nowhere seemed to put something back into sync in me. I blinked at her and knew who she was. "Oh," I said. "Hi, Rawnie."

"Yo, Harper." She looked me over like she was checking to make sure I had my fly zipped or something. "Where's your harp?"

She was making one of her straight-faced little jokes. But I really felt like I should have a harp, like I'd left it somewhere, and where was it?

"Come on," I said, and took a few steps. The deer snorted and menaced with its antlers.

"Whoa!" Rawnie exclaimed, grabbing at my arm. "Those are sharper than spears."

"Let us pass," I said to the deer. "I am the daughter of Aengus Mac Og. Let us pass." It looked at me for a moment, then stood back and cleared the way.

I looked at Rawnie and asked her, "You ready for this?" We both knew we might never come out. Once a person goes into that place, they're not supposed to come back.

"I might not ever be ready," Rawnie said, "but let's do it anyway."

We walked to where the shadowy path began and knew right away that we still had a long way to go. There were bouncers everywhere. The first one was Gus's old gas pump. I mean, I knew it was the gas pump, just as I knew the deer was the pipe-and-pitchfork deer from her front yard. But that didn't mean the deer couldn't spear us with its horns, and it didn't mean the gas pump couldn't stop us either. It was a tall white lady with a round glass head, and she said to us in a rusty voice, "Tickets. You need tickets to get in here."

"C'mon," I whispered to Rawnie, and we ran past her. But she had rubber arms ten feet long, and they shot out like tentacles and snapped around our waists with her heavy steel hands hitting our backs. We screamed and spun our way out of them and kept running and ran into somebody or something else that laughed like a machine and had a face like a carnival freak and threw the long shadows of its uplifted hands on the ground. We screamed again and knocked it

over, getting away. Then we ran like rabbits. Half a
minute later, though, we knew we were lost and had
to stop and stand and listen, panting.

The band was playing, "Walk tall, walk tall, into the
darkness of the longest night of all."

"That way," Rawnie puffed, and we headed toward
the music, trying to do what it said. Which was hard
because at the same time we tried to stay in the shadows and dodge the bouncers. Some of them were just
regular people patrolling the place, a lot like the security guards at the Arena except I knew that in day-
light and in my right mind I wouldn't have been able
to see them. Maybe feel their hands pushing me away
from places I wasn't supposed to be, yes, but not see
them. There were other kinds of security guards too.
Rawnie and I saw a Chinese dragon snorting fire
through its metal nostrils, a giant pigeon flying over
with eyes that glowed like night-lights, a shadow that
grew hands. No wonder nobody bothered Gus's prop-
erty. Aengus Mac Og's backyard was full of guardians
to keep the living out.

"This yard is bigger than it should be," I whispered
to Rawnie after a while. It was taking us forever to get
to the creek, and not just because we were sneaking
either.

"Sh. I don't want to hear it, Harper."

I didn't shush, because I saw something glimmer-
ing up ahead. "Look. There's water. And it's bigger
than it should be too."

It sure was. The creek had turned the size of a
river, not the Mississippi or anything but plenty too
big to just jump across. There it lay like tar under

the black sky, and Rawnie and I stood at the edge looking at it. All through the water we could see goldfish shining like beer signs in bar windows at midnight.

"Maybe it's not too deep," I said after a while, and I stuck one foot in to find out. Then I hollered. The water was cold enough to freeze your bones, but that wasn't what made me scream—something rushed me. As soon as my foot touched the water there was a swirl and a splash and a flash of goldfish scales as something hit my toes. I jumped back so fast I fell down on the grass.

"Harper! You all right?" Rawnie was so scared she forgot to be quiet.

I sat up to find out. "Look," I said. The front inch of my shoe was gone. Those so-called goldfish had bitten straight through canvas and rubber and everything. My toes stuck out of the hole. At least they weren't hurt.

"Radical," Rawnie declared. "We can forget wading across."

Then another splashing noise turned her around. This one was water slapping against metal. A boat was coming toward us over the black water.

"Run!" I scrambled up. But Rawnie stood still.

"No, better stay," she said. "How else are we supposed to get across?"

She was right. So we stood still and waited.

It was just an aluminum rowboat with its nose up in the air, the way Aly Bowman always kept hers. A big man sat in the back of the boat and paddled it. His paddle looked awfully familiar. So did he, and when I got a good look at him I moaned. The man was Mr. Kuchwald.

"That's it," I said to Rawnie, only half joking. "I'm going home."

"I have a feeling we couldn't get out of here now if we wanted to."

Which we didn't want to, not really, because of Nico.

Mr. Kuchwald scooted the boat's nose up on the bank right by us, and it stuck there. "Gold for the boatman," he said.

We didn't understand. "Um," Rawnie said to him, "will you take us across the river?"

"Of course." He showed his teeth. "For a fee. Gold for the boatman."

"But we don't—"

"You don't have anything for me? Then you will wander here for eternity. So think. You must have something."

Rawnie took the gold studs out of her ears and offered them to him. Mr. Kuchwald—I guess it wasn't really Mr. Kuchwald—shook his head. "Not enough."

I tried to think, like he said. There was no gold on me. I didn't have on anything valuable, not a watch, not any jewelry except . . .

I fingered my necklace. It wasn't gold, but it was worth a chunk of gold to me. I glanced at Rawnie, and she nodded.

"We've got to," she said, and she helped me with the clasp. She took mine off me and I took hers off her. Then I handed them both to the boatman.

"They're not gold," I said, "but they're valuable."

He fitted the pendants together and nodded. "Yes," he said, "a yang-yin. They certainly are. Step in."

Five minutes later we were on the opposite shore. The boat had left us there and gone away over the dark water again. We stood for a minute watching it go. My hand kept going to the emptiness at my neck where my friendship necklace wasn't anymore.

"It's all right, Harper," Rawnie told me. "We don't need them. We know who we are."

CHAPTER NINE

♪

"I'm tired," Rawnie said. She was not complaining, just saying it.

"No kidding."

"I'm hungry too."

Now that we were in the maze, it no longer felt like we were outside. I didn't remember going through a wall or a door, but I couldn't see the sky or hear the music except as a muffled sort of thumping that seemed to come from everywhere, and there were walls to each side of us, metal ones. There was some light, but I couldn't tell where it was coming from. It was like being in a sewer. No, more like being lost in a mess of basement corridors in some huge new school. Except that we weren't lost really. I knew where I was, I knew my way through the maze in Gus's backyard. It was just that everything seemed different and so much bigger. Our footsteps echoed. So did Rawnie's voice saying she was hungry—hungry—hungry . . .

"I'm not," I told her.

"We've been in here for hours." (Hours—hours—hours ...)

"It just feels like hours."

"Anyway, you've gotta be hungry."

"I'm not. I'm too starved to be just hungry."

"Okay, be that way. What's that smell?"

All of a sudden we were drowning in a drooler, a stomach-growler of a good food smell, and I didn't even have time to think up a smart-mouth answer for Rawnie before we turned a corner and there it was.

"A hot dog stand!"

Wow, were they ever hot dogs. Plump, brick-red foot-longs sizzling on their grill. Not a bit like the wimpy green hot dogs at school. Though by then I was so starved I could have gobbled down anything, even school food.

"Free hot dogs," the person behind the counter told us politely. She had a pale face and not much hair but she did have a big beak of a nose, which she talked through. "As many as you like." She offered us one in each hand.

"All *riiiiight!*" Rawnie started to reach for one, but I grabbed her arm.

"Listen, there's no hot dog stand in Gus's backyard."

"So what? There is now!" She pulled her arm away from me, but I got hold of the other one, because I had a funny feeling.

"No, wait, Rawnie, don't!" My stomach was growling maybe even louder than hers, but I never did trust anything that was free. Also, there was something about the hot dog lady—I should know her. I didn't like her, and why did I keep thinking about school?

"Free," White-face urged, poking hot dogs toward us. Her pale hands had long fingernails painted black.

"Let me go!" Rawnie squirmed away from me, but I lunged after her and got her by both arms from behind.

"Harper, stop it!"

"No, Rawnie, listen, it's some sort of a trap!"

She wasn't listening. I found out later that the one way to make Rawnie go absolutely psycho was to grab her from behind. Always, ever since she was a little kid, it made her fight like a wildcat. Which was what she did. She elbowed me in the ribs so hard that everything went black for a second. I doubled over, and I guess my hands slipped. She twisted around and tore loose and hit me in the face with her fist. That girl really knew how to hit. I had to stagger back or I would have fallen over.

"You don't tell me what to do!" she screamed at me. She stood panting at me a minute, and then she turned away and headed toward the hot dogs again.

My ribs hurt and my head hurt clear down to my knees and I was so shaking mad at her that I nearly let her do it. It still scares me, remembering the way I felt for a second. But something else took over. My heart made my feet get moving, and I ran and tackled Rawnie before she got far. This time I didn't mess around. I knocked her flat on the ground and sat on top of her. She struggled and tried to throw me off, but I outweighed her.

"Damn it, Harper, get off me! You big moose, I hate you!"

I knew she didn't mean it, and I wasn't listening anyway. I was staring up at the hot dog lady, trying to know for sure who she was. She hadn't moved, which was weird. She was still standing behind her counter with her arms stretched out like black wings. "Free," she crooned. She looked at me.

"Go away, Aly," I told her.

When Rawnie heard that, she stopped fighting me, went stiff instead, and turned her head to look. But I didn't have time to say anything to her before the hot dog nearest to us changed and started to wiggle out of its bun. It was a fat night crawler, falling toward us.

"Ew!" You better believe I got off Rawnie fast. She grabbed my hand and scrambled up.

The whole hot dog stand was melting, and the hot dogs were turning into worms, and they were crawling on the ground, or floor, whatever it was, and the woman was saying, "Scree!" instead of "Free." She was a vulture, mostly, a black buzzard with a six-foot wingspread and road-kill breath. Her bald head had spiral-perm blond bangs that curled down over her beak. She pecked at the nearest worm to gobble it and grabbed another with one of her scaly clawed feet.

Rawnie made a retching noise, then turned and ran. I ran after her. "Wait up," I panted. My ribs still hurt, and I never could run as fast as she did anyway.

Once we were around a corner she stopped and waited for me. When I caught up to her I felt so dizzy

I had to lean against the wall with my eyes closed while I caught my breath.

Rawnie said, "Harper, you all right?"

I nodded.

"Jeez, I gave you a black eye." Her voice sounded shaky. "God, Harper, I'm really sorry."

"You don't ever have to tell me you're sorry for anything." The words just came out, I didn't have to think about them, and they were true. I opened my eyes to look at her, and she looked back and swallowed hard and nodded.

I got myself moving, and we kept walking.

"How did you know it was Alabaster?" Rawnie asked after a while.

"I dunno. I mean, it wasn't her exactly."

"Okay, so we're not exactly in Gus's backyard either. But how did you know it was sort of her?"

"I just guessed." There were about three ways of looking at anything in this shadowland, so maybe if I went back and looked at the vulture again it wouldn't be Aly. Not that I was going back. I told Rawnie, "Mostly, I just don't think we should eat anything."

She shivered. "I'd rather die than take food from her."

"No matter who offers it. Even if we're both starving, we shouldn't take any."

I couldn't have explained why, because I didn't know the reason. It was just a feeling I had, like I'd been in this sort of place once before with a harp in my hand. Like I knew some of the rules.

Rawnie didn't ask me why, though. She just looked at me and said, "Okay. I won't forget again."

"Huh?" It was not as if I'd told her before. "Forget what?"

"Who my friend is."

We kept walking. Running away from the Aly Bowman buzzard had got us all turned around, and neither of us knew anymore which direction we were heading.

I was plodding more than walking. "You okay, Harper?" Rawnie asked me after a while.

My eye hurt and made my head throb. Also my ribs hurt. But I said, "I'm just dead tired. I wish we would find Nico soon."

Rawnie slowed down and pointed up ahead. "Look," she said. "Light."

And there they were, the stage lights, all colors, and we could hear the music again, so strong and beautiful that I didn't care anymore if I was tired and hurting and hungry. I looked at Rawnie and smiled.

A couple minutes later we came out of the maze. We were in the circle at its center, where rows of seats faced a stage with a big red drum riser on it. Behind the big red platform was a wall with a huge circle design that kept turning, turning, white and black and black and white. The music was like the circle, it just went around and around, and kept coming.

We said, Hey, Daddy, we're not about to die
'Cause living is the truth and death is a lie.
So rock it, rock it, just rock it on by,
Big wheel turns and the stars keep burning.

It was like they were playing just for themselves, or us. We could have any seat we wanted, front row if we wanted, because there was nobody in the audience. Everybody was onstage.

We didn't sit down, though, but just stood staring.

"This is so intense," Rawnie whispered. "They are so *hot.*"

"Hot as Neon Shadow."

"Hotter!"

Some of them were on the riser with the drummer and his congas and cymbals and things, they were up there playing wild fills and fast runs like guitar gods on a mountaintop, and some of them were all around the red—I knew it was the red car—on keyboard and sax and tambourines, and they were all young, they were all rocking, they were all beautiful one way or another. But it wasn't so much their faces or the way they moved or the way they were dressed that made me want to scream and faint and turn inside out. Or even the way they sang, though they were singing like fire. It was just that they were so alive.

I blurted at Rawnie or whatever would listen, "These are *dead* dudes? These can't be dead people."

They weren't ghosts or anything like that. They looked as solid as I was. Yet they weren't quite real, I knew that. They were too perfect. The lead singer, the one at the center mike, he had a face like a bad angel. He was like a baby-faced desperado, an outlaw throwing his body at the world, but there was something about him that made me think of an orphan at the same time, like I wanted to take him and cuddle him and calm him down and make him smile.

"They're dead, all right," Rawnie said softly. "Because there's Elvis, and he's young again."

"Oh, my God." Now I understood why people had cried when he died. "That's Elvis?"

"Yepper."

"Oh, my God. Who are these other guys, then? Who's the one in glasses?"

"I don't know."

"Buddy Holly," said a quiet voice behind us. "Horn-rims and a Stratocaster. There's never been anybody quite like him."

The band roared, "Rock it! Rock it! Rock it on by. . . ."

Already—even before I turned around—I knew. And there he stood, right next to me. Nico Torres.

"Because living is the truth and death is a lie."

But it wasn't all of Nico, really. He was half made of air. I could see through him. The rest of him was still unconscious in a hospital bed.

"Nico!" Rawnie and I both screeched.

"You know me?" His face was a lot like Rawnie's, dark and beautiful and real quiet whenever he was not singing. It hardly moved even when we screamed at him. I could tell he was surprised, though. "Who are you guys? So far nobody knows me here."

"We're not from here!" Rawnie had to do the explaining, because I was having trouble getting my mouth coordinated enough to talk. "We came to find you and take you back with us."

"Why?" He hardly even seemed interested. His eyes were on the band, and he said, "My God, look at Hendrix bend those strings."

"Because we love you," Rawnie said. "We think you're the greatest."

He didn't even smile, just said, "I'm not. These guys are the greatest. Hendrix taught the whole world how to turn on the juice. So did Elvis, he took rock music out of its little black box and turned it loose. And Morrison, look at him grooving with his shirt off, he was half-crazy, he died young and stupid, but he knew how to rock and he knew how to sing. Still does. And Lennon—he wrote songs people can't forget."

My voice was starting to work again. "Nico," I said, "you've got to come back with us."

"Why?" His eyes focused on me, and they were deep, like brown water, and not happy. "Give me one good reason."

"To be alive!"

"Tell me something, what is so great about being alive? I thought I had a friend, and now that I'm in trouble all he can think about is cashing in. He left me on my own, I've always been all alone and I'll always be all alone, but here at least I could be in the ultimate band."

He was as ultimate as any of them, so drop-dead good-looking I could hardly bear to stand next to him and talk to him, but at the same time I started to understand something else about him. Underneath all the rock star stuff, he was just a kid, not much older than me. Not that much different than the boys at my school. He was feeling sorry for himself. Probably he got pimples every once in a while too, and hated them. Which didn't make me stop liking him. In fact I think it made me like him more. But in a different way than before.

"Somebody's been beating on you too," he said to me, looking at my shiner.

"Not really. Nico, being alive is—is—"

"To dance," Rawnie said. "To sing."

"I can do that here. Janis Joplin was here a while ago. You should have heard her sing."

"To make your own songs."

He sat down in one of the metal chairs as if to say he wasn't moving. "I can do that here too. Del Shannon's already written a dozen good ones since he's been here."

This wasn't working. "Look," I said, sitting down next to him, "I know it was rough, what Ty did to you. And I know probably we don't really understand, we're just a couple of sixth-grade girls, but—"

"Just?" He looked at me, and the way he did it made me stop talking, because there was something warm and bright starting in his eyes. "What do you mean, just girls? Don't you know girls are the most awesome thing there is? You've got such a mystery about you. Sometimes I think girls know more about life the day they're born than guys ever learn."

Rawnie sat down on the other side of Nico, and I guess we were both staring at him, and he actually smiled.

"You two, you're girlfriends, right?" he said. We both nodded. "Okay, right there you got something most guys never get. I thought I had it with Ty. . . ." He lost his smile. "Thing is, guys don't know how to be friends, not really. We don't really talk with each other.

There's a lot of stuff we never say, afraid we'll look like sissies or something. We're always competing with each other. Look at them." He pointed his chin at the rockers on stage. "Elvis is hogging the mike again, and they're all just waiting for a chance to get it away from him. Sometimes they act real buddy-buddy, but they'd walk over each other to get what they want."

I looked at the rock stars on stage. They were all singing together, all dancing and stomping to the music. They looked wonderful to me, like a team, a gang, pals. Were they really alone inside themselves? Each one wanting to be the one at the mike?

Maybe they were. Nico was a guy, he should know what it was really like.

I said half to myself, "I always thought it was better to be a boy."

"God, no. A guy has to always be trying to prove something. Look at the way jocks act. Hugging each other on the field, giving each other hell in the locker room."

"Nico," Rawnie said softly, "don't give up on Ty."

"I don't want to give up, but I got to, girl. He gave up on me."

"Maybe he doesn't see it that way. Maybe he thinks he's doing what he has to do."

"Sure, he thinks he's got to, but that doesn't help me." Nico took a breath and tried to explain. "The thing is, maybe he's got his own agenda, maybe it's important to him to be a star without me. But where does that leave me? What about the way I feel?"

I said, "You mean that you really liked him, and you thought you'd always be together."

Nico didn't answer me for a minute. He was looking at me as if something was a little off-key. Then he said, "Do you know, 'The Friendship Song'?"

I had to smile. Rawnie was looking at me and smiling too. Did we know "The Friendship Song"? Jeez. But all we said was, "Uh-huh."

Nico said, "I love that song."

"So do we," I told him.

"Not just like it's a happenin' song. I mean I really love it."

"So do we."

"Do you really know what I'm saying?"

I thought I did. In fact, I knew all along. "You're saying you *meant* it when you sang it."

"Yeah. Yes. I really did, I really believed it. I sang it with my heart hanging out." He gave us a look that was partly angry but mostly hurt. Way bad hurt. There were tears in his eyes. "Well, so much for that, huh? Now what?"

So much for Rawnie and Harper, Rescuers, Inc. There wasn't a thing we could do or say. We didn't have an answer for him.

CHAPTER
TEN
♪

The ultimate band kept playing while the lights flashed all the colors in the world and the big circle behind the drum stand kept turning around and around. For a long time Nico and Rawnie and I sat in the music like sitting in the sun, talking. Nico was like Rawnie and me, he had this feeling of the way things should be, the way people should be good to each other. We talked about a lot of things. But we couldn't talk him into coming back with us.

"Look, I'll think about it," was the best answer we got from him. "It's the least I can do, when you two kids came in here after me—"

He stopped talking and looked at us with a strange, worried shadow starting in his eyes.

"What?" Rawnie asked him.

"Jeez," he said softly, "now I know I'm far gone. Here I sit just thinking about myself, and what about you two? How are you going to get back?"

Rawnie groaned. I rolled my eyes. "Through the maze again, I guess," I said.

"I don't want to think about it," Rawnie said. "And I'm so hungry."

Nico exclaimed, "You didn't eat anything in here, did you?"

"No."

"Good. Don't! If you eat anything, you can't leave."

Rawnie looked at me like she wanted to say something that didn't need saying. And I just wanted to change the subject anyway. I said, "I wonder what day it is."

"Isn't it still the same night?" Rawnie looked startled.

"How should I know? It feels like we've been in here a week."

"You can't go out the way you came in," Nico said. "The boatman won't take you." He was keeping his voice very quiet, but I could tell he was scared. As if it was his fault we were in there. It wasn't. He couldn't help it if we came in after him. But he cared about us. That was the kind of person he was.

He was right too. That boatman was just the kind of person who wouldn't take us back across the creek. Now I was scared. "Oh, my God," I said to Rawnie, and the way she was looking at me didn't help.

We all three sat like spare tires for a minute.

"How do you get in and out?" I asked Nico.

"I fly."

Forget it. That wouldn't work for Rawnie and me. We sat some more.

"We sort of got in by letting the music take us," Rawnie said, not sounding too sure of herself. "Maybe we can get out by not letting it have us anymore?"

"Put your hands over your ears," Nico told us, "and think about going home."

"What about you?"

"Forget me. Do it."

I tried it and knew right away it wasn't going to work. I could still hear the music. Or what I mean is, the music was still in me, right down to my bones, the way there was always music in Rawnie's feet. I could feel it like I could feel my heartbeat. And deep down I didn't want to make it stop. It would be like dying if I made it stop. I needed to have it with me always.

"Think about summertime coming," Nico was saying. "Think about, oh, I don't know, things you like to eat. Petting a cat, walking a dog. Hanging out with people you really like." His voice was starting to quiver. "Brothers, sisters, father, mother. People who love you."

I wanted all that, but I wanted the music too.

"Nico," said Rawnie very gently, "come with us."

"Give me a break and just get yourselves home, okay?" His voice was stretched tight as a drumhead.

"We don't know how," she said.

"Yes, we do," I told her. I had gone kind of fuzzy because I was so tired and hungry, or I would have thought of it before. "The other way. By the pigeon coop."

"Yeah!" She understood. "The back way! But where is it?"

"I see what you mean," Nico said. "There ought to be a stage door."

He got up and headed toward where he thought it might be. Rawnie and I trailed along behind him.

"Jeez," I muttered, surprised at how tired and old I felt.

Nico walked up onstage, and so did we, and Elvis kept jumping around and singing "Rock it, rock it," but Buddy Holly stopped banging out the beat on his old Stratocaster and looked at us.

"Hey," he said. "People. Kids. Girls."

"Quite so, that's what they are," said Lennon. He was standing there playing a big mouthful of shiny metal, a harmonica. He smiled at us around the edges of it, then kept playing, and I was glad. I wanted the music never to end.

"They need to go home," Nico said. "They're not dead."

"They ought to see the manager," Buddy Holly said. He was dressed in a white nerd shirt and black nerd slacks, not like any rock star I had ever dreamed of. The only halfway cool thing he had on was a belt with a big silver lonesome-cowboy buckle. Actually it was kind of old-fashioned-looking, and I never was much for cowboy stuff. But I liked him anyway. He seemed nice. Not just smiley nice, but nice all the way to his bones.

"What about you, kid?" he said to Nico. "Made up your mind yet?"

"No," Nico said.

"Listen, y'all go back, then. Take it from me, never die young. It's not worth it. Being a dead rock legend sucks."

I saw Nico's eyes go wide. But all he said was, "Where do we find the manager?"

"Where do you think?" somebody else shouted

over. It was Hendrix, and he sounded mad that we were interrupting things. "Backstage!"

See, the strange thing was, even though I knew we were in Gus's backyard, it was like we were in a stadium or an arena. There were walls. And I looked to the right and I looked to the left, but I didn't see any doors in them.

"How do we get there?" Nico asked.

Nobody answered him. Maybe nobody heard, because the band was swinging into "Born to Be Wild," Buddy Holly was hitting the strings hard, John Lennon was swaying to the beat, drums were pounding, the lights were flashing blue and purple and bloodred, and I laughed out loud, because suddenly I saw. I grabbed Nico with one hand, Rawnie with the other.

"Step in," I told them. "Step into the circle."

Right in front of us, big, was the backdrop with the circle that kept turning. And I had been thinking its black-and-white design was yang and yin, but watching the colors hit it all at once, I saw it in a different way. With the lights on it, it was the hex sign from the pigeon coop. And if things could come through it to make the band play, maybe we could go through it the other way.

"Come on," I urged. "It's the hex."

Something strange was happening. The music was dwindling away like into the distance, and light was coming from somewhere, everything was getting bright. The circle blazed like fire. "What's happening?" Rawnie exclaimed, holding me back.

"Night's ending," Nico said. "Gig's nearly over. Get going, you two." He pulled his hand out of mine.

"Nico, come with us!"

"I don't *know* what to do! Stop thinking about me and just go!" One hand on each of us between the shoulder blades, he gave us a shove that should have sent us slamming off the stage and into the wall behind it.

But the stage did not end when it should have. We fell into the slowly spinning circle, I fell into yang and Rawnie fell into yin, or it might have been the other way around, it didn't matter. Then we weren't falling anymore, we were floating or drifting or spinning, backstage, behind everything, the two of us.

And then we were face to face with the manager of eternity's band.

"Harper," he said, "what are you doing here?"

He knew me. And I felt like I should know him, but I wasn't sure who he was, and I couldn't think, because he was so—he was hot, like the sun. His face was young and handsome and almost golden; it seemed to shine. His hair was long and thick and flowed back from his face like a lion's mane and formed a circle in the sky. His eyes—they were so bright I couldn't look at his face after the first glimpse, and I felt Rawnie's hand tighten on mine like she needed something to hang on to.

"Daughter," the golden man said. "What are you doing here?"

There was some kind of mistake. I whispered, "I'm not your daughter."

"But you told my gatekeeper you were."

Oh, my God. Aengus Mac Og.

He was right. I nodded. "Yes, okay, I remember. I was thinking of Gus. She's—she's real nice, I wouldn't mind if she wanted to be my mom. But I haven't had a chance to talk with her about it yet." Aengus Mac Og and Gus were not exactly the same person, I could see that now. I mean, obviously Aengus Mac Og was a man and Gus was a woman, but it was more than just that. It was—Gus was Gus. She was born in a real place, Youngstown, Ohio. In a real year, even though I didn't know what it was. She went to Iowa State University, she protested the Vietnam War, she could never get a good job because she wouldn't shave her legs and wear high heels. She had a birth certificate and someday she would die. But Aengus Mac Og would never die, and he was a lot more powerful and a lot scarier than Gus would ever be.

"Answer my question," he commanded. "What treasure have you and your comrade come to steal from me?"

"We, uh, we came to take Nico."

"The one who wavers between the worlds. Nico Torres."

"Yes. But it was a mistake to try, we can't make him come back, we don't own him, we can't tell him what to do. . . ." My voice faltered as I remembered the feel of Nico's hand pulling out of mine.

"He will make his own decision. And you wish to go back to the world of the living?"

"Yes. Yes, sir."

"And you are taking with you nothing you have found here?"

"No."

"Do not trifle with me. I know you have stolen treasure from my realm."

Aengus Mac Og sounded very stern. I looked at Rawnie before I answered, and she looked back at me. Had we taken something, maybe by mistake? She shook her head. I couldn't remember anything either.

Except—there had been music I didn't want to leave behind.

"The music," I said, "It's in me now. Is that what you mean, sir?"

"How is it in you, Harper?" And now his voice had gone softer.

"It's—like my own song. A dream." I couldn't explain any better than that, and maybe Aengus Mac Og didn't understand. Or maybe he did. I don't know, because I wasn't looking at him, I was looking at Rawnie, and she understood all right. It was as if she and I were partners in something. On the same team. And either one of us alone wasn't a bad deal, but put us together and we were more than twice as strong, we could be heroes, poets, whatever we wanted. Our hands curled together like yang and yin, and we lifted them into the air. Our arms made a shape like a mountain peak. We were adventurers, and we would ride together. We were gladiators, and we had both won. Rawnie smiled at me, and there was a tear on her cheek. It shone there like a jewel, just like she was somebody. Just like we were rock stars or something.

"I see," Aengus Mac Og said, and his voice sounded gentle and proud. "It is a treasure you have earned. Take it, therefore, and go."

Then before I had time to think or be afraid the sky behind his head was a circle that grew, and flew toward us, and swallowed us up and spun us around. "Hey!" I yelled. Rawnie's hand hung on to mine. Then everything was very still, and life smelled like a spring morning, and I blinked: We were sitting on the grass by a pile of old buckets and hubcaps, and Gus was standing there looking down at us with those dreaming gray eyes of hers. The sun was shining bright and golden, and there was a circle hanging like a halo behind Gus's head, but it was just the hex sign on the pigeon coop.

Next thing I knew I got up and grabbed her around the middle and started to cry into the bib of her overalls.

"Groover!" Her hands came up and hugged me and patted at me. "What is it, buddy?"

"Nico," I managed to blurt out, and then I couldn't say anymore, but I guess she understood. I was crying because the world was beautiful and I was back in it—and Nico was not. The sun was warm, but Nico was still flying in the wind somewhere.

CHAPTER
ELEVEN
♪

Gus knew what was going on, of course, but there was no way we could explain to my father or Rawnie's father how we'd been up all night trying to rescue Nico from shadowland. So after I was done crying on Gus, Rawnie had to sneak into her house and I had to sneak into mine, and we each had to go to bed for all of ten minutes and pretend we had been there all along and get up and get ready for school.

"How'd you get the black eye?" Dad wanted to know the minute he saw me, which was when I walked into the kitchen for breakfast.

I surprised him, because instead of answering I went over to him and gave him a big hug and a kiss and rested my head on him a minute. After the way I'd been hugging Gus, I guess I felt like he should get equal time. "Dad," I told him, still hugging him, "I need new sneaks. One of mine got the toe whomped off." I swung up my foot to show him. "And I need a bra, sometime soon," I added.

Gus sloshed her coffee all over the table and

gawked at me. "Criminy," she said. "I never thought of that."

I grinned at her. "You're gonna be my mom, you have to think of these things."

She heard what I was trying to tell her, and she smiled back at me like a big pink sunrise.

Dad's coffee was still brewing, so he was cranky and he was missing half of this. "What did you do to your shoe?" he wanted to know. "And you still didn't tell me what happened to your eye."

I could have made up a lie, I guess, but I didn't feel like it. I let go of him and looked straight at him and said, "I'm not going to."

"What?"

"Dad, it's private."

"You got in a fight and you're not going to tell me about it?"

"That's right." He was starting to look mad, so I said, "Dad, suppose I was a boy, would it bother you? Girls can do things too."

Gus was watching him in her quiet way, and he felt it and stared back at her. "You in on this?"

"Yes."

He flapped his hands in the air and gave up. "All right, then. Harper, what you don't tell me, you tell Gus. You hear me?"

"Okay. Hey, Dad. Thanks for marrying Gus."

He smiled, and tried to hide it, and stomped over to get his coffee. "I hate Mondays," he muttered.

Rawnie said pretty much the same thing on the way to school. "And it's Monday, yet," she moaned as we headed down the street. "If we live through this, we can live through anything." For once her feet weren't dancing. She was almost dragging them. And I was walking like a drunk moose.

I had my Walkman, and most of the way to school we listened for news of Nico. We didn't talk much about him, though. What could we say? It was all up to him now, whether he lived or died. We couldn't talk to him, even to say good-bye. He could be walking right by my side now and I wouldn't know it, because he was in the air like a distant song. I couldn't see him or hear him anymore.

There was no change in the news about him.

"If he decides to come back," I said to Rawnie, "probably he won't remember anything."

"I guess not."

"But that's okay. It doesn't matter if he doesn't remember us. Just if he comes back."

"Yeah."

"Please come back, Nico."

Some time that morning, I really don't remember when, Aly Bowman came up to me and said in my face, hard, "You sitting with me at lunch today?" I stood in the hall blinking at her. So much had happened that it was like I barely remembered who she was, like she was somebody I knew for a little while a long time ago and now I couldn't think of her name, but it didn't matter. I knew she wasn't anyone I wanted to eat lunch with.

"No," I said.

"What do you mean, no?"

"I mean, no. I'm sitting with Rawnie."

"Butch bitch." The way it came out so fast I could see she had already thought of what names she was going to call me. "You are a big overgrown butch, Harper."

She walked away just as I remembered who she was. "Hey, Aly," I called after her, "you've got green worms hanging down from your beak. Juicy ones."

She shot me a killer look over her shoulder. "I'll get you," she said.

I didn't care about that or what she'd called me, because she just wasn't important.

Nico was way bad important. But when I met Rawnie for lunch, there was still no news about him.

I wanted Nico to get well so hard that I wasn't thinking about much else. Or maybe it was because I was so tired I just didn't care anymore. Or maybe it was more like, I didn't *scare* anymore. Anyway, I didn't tell Rawnie about Aly, I didn't worry about the glares she was giving me or the way she was whispering with her boyfriend, and for some reason I wasn't carrying my books in front of my chest that day. I just didn't feel like it. They were so heavy. My arms always ached after a day of going around that way. And why should I have to, anyhow?

Right after lunch, when everybody was sloshing around in the lobby like clothes in a real noisy washing machine, a hand came grabbing straight for the front of my sweatshirt.

I didn't even wait to see who it was, I didn't even think about what to do, I just punched for all I was worth. Rawnie was standing right beside me, and she hit him the same time I did. Between the two of us, we flattened him pretty good. Then all of a sudden there was a circle of space around us and kids staring at us. We didn't try to sneak away or anything, we just stood there looking at the boy getting up off the floor. It wasn't Brent this time, it was somebody else, some skinhead boy I didn't even know. His nose was bleeding, but I couldn't feel sorry for him.

"Young ladies," Mr. Kuchwald roared in our ears, "to my office!"

He didn't say anything until we got there, but I could hear him breathing hard, like he was really mad and not just putting on an act. Rawnie and I just looked at each other and didn't say anything. We didn't have to. I was scared, but it was okay, because in another secret way I wasn't scared at all. It was like I was just me, but I was more than just me when I had to be.

Like "The Friendship Song" in one way was just a song, and Nico and Ty were just singers, they had never really died for each other. But in another way the song was true.

Mr. Kuchwald waited until he had Rawnie and me in his office with the door closed before he said anything. But then he turned straight to me. "*You,*" he yelled, pointing his finger almost into my face. "Here you are in my office again, for fighting, just the way you were the very first day you set foot in my school."

He'd promised he was going to forget that. But I didn't remind him, because there was something more important to say.

I looked straight at him and I told him, "Mr. Kuch-wald, that boy grabbed my breast."

"What!" His face turned red, and his voice went squeaky. He seemed madder than ever. It looked to me like I was just getting myself into deeper trouble, but too bad. I wasn't sorry for anything.

"He grabbed her breast," Rawnie said. "That's what Brent did to her too."

"And if anybody does it again, I am going to hit him again," I said. Not loud or hard. I just said it.

"You are *not,*" Mr. Kuchwald snapped. "You are going to come straight here and tell me, and I will hit him myself." He paced fast twice around the room like he was going a little crazy. "Why doesn't anybody tell me these things are going on?" he burst out. "Once garbage like this gets started, it's hard to stop. If some-body would *tell* me what's happening, I could do something."

He didn't seem to really be talking to Rawnie or me, so we didn't say anything. But I was thinking, why should it be right for him to hit a kid and not right for me? If a boy touched me in the wrong place, I sure wasn't going to just say, Stop it, I'm telling. I was going to at least shove him away. Hard.

Mr. Kuchwald was mad, all right. He was boiling. But I could see now it wasn't exactly at Rawnie and me. He circled around once more, then sat down be-hind his desk, which was a good sign. He looked at us.

"I am going to give you two detention," he said. "But I want to tell you this, a certain boy is going to get more than just detention. In fact I can think of a couple of boys with whom I am going to have a couple of long and heartfelt talks."

"Okay," I said.

"Good," Rawnie said.

"Do you two have anything else you need to tell me?"

"I don't think so," Rawnie said.

But I was looking at Mr. Kuchwald's desk. Something familiar was lying on top of it. Two things. "Mr. Kuchwald," I said, "that's my necklace, and the other one is Rawnie's."

He looked at them as though he'd never seen them before. "Where did those come from? I can't remember where I picked them up. Did I take them away from you for something?"

We just looked at him and smiled.

He rolled his eyes. "You girls do not want me to have a very good day, do you?" he complained. "Okay, have them back." He handed our friendship necklaces to us. "And stay out of my office, you hear? No more hitting."

"Not unless I have to," I told him, and he stared hard at me but he didn't say anything.

"Bye," Rawnie told him, all sunshine.

When we got back out in the hall we looked at each other and grinned like lions, because we had won. Then we put our necklaces on.

When we finally walked home that day we were so tired it was like we were floating on a river of air. My Walkman wouldn't work, and that kind of sent us over the edge. We got silly. Our feet moved, but our heads didn't seem connected to them in any way. We trickled down the sidewalks like water. Sometimes we stopped for a few minutes before we remembered who we were and where we were and started moving again.

Gus was out on the porch waiting, and when she saw us waver into sight she got up and walked to meet us. Really, she didn't just walk. She hurried, she almost ran. It was about the fastest I'd ever seen her move except maybe the time she jumped over the U-Haul hood to kiss my dad.

"You coming to prop us up?" Rawnie called. She wasn't a bit scared of Gus anymore.

"Sure, I'll do that." She put an arm around each of us and steered us down the street. "But what I really want is to tell you what I just heard on the radio."

Even before she said it we both knew, and we both started jumping like we weren't dead tired after all, and we both screamed, "Nico!"

It was true. Nico Torres was conscious. Out of danger. Off the critical list. Asking for a pencil and a piece of paper so he could write down an idea for a song.

A week passed. It took most of it for Rawnie and me to stop feeling tired.

Gus found the exact right thing to go with her flagpole eagle and license plate and smashed Pepsi can, which was a silver belt buckle shaped like a lonesome cowboy with a guitar on his back. She found it just lying on the ground, out near the red drum riser— I mean, the red Cadillac.

Dad took me shopping for new shoes, and he

nailed the old ones up on a big tree in the backyard to start a "shoe tree." He nailed up his oldest pair too, and a pair of Gus's. From now on all our old shoes would go up there together, because we were a family.

Rawnie didn't tear up her pictures of Ty Shaney, but she did put them all away in the back of her closet.

I didn't have any more trouble in school. Aly Bowman was trying to make some, she went around telling everybody I was an overgrown butch, but who cared? Nobody who mattered listened to Aly. Anyway, I didn't mind anymore that I'm big. If a person is going to try to be a rock guitarist, it's a good idea to be big and tall.

The most important thing that happened was, by the end of the week Nico Torres was moved out of intensive care into a regular hospital room.

Saturday we went to visit him. It was Gus's idea. Rawnie and I would never have tried it ourselves. How could we expect to get in, past all the security and stuff? But Gus told us, "No problem." And sure enough, when she said her name to the guard at the hospital elevator, the man got on his walkie-talkie and word came back from someplace to let us come on up.

Nico was sitting in bed with a big pillow behind his head when we came into the room. He looked pale. Being so near to him made my heart ache, and I couldn't stop staring at him, but it didn't matter. He wasn't looking at me or Rawnie, just at Gus.

"Uh, Gus McCogg?"

"Yeppers. That's me."

"Um, jeez, I've got it all wrong. I was expecting a guy. Uh—you're really him? I mean, uh, her? You're the Gus McCogg who wrote 'The Friendship Song'?"

The answer was yes. I don't remember the words exactly because my mouth had dropped open so far my jaw tripped some sort of circuit breaker in my brain and I wasn't functioning. All I could do was babble. "Ba-ba-bu-but—"

"You?" Rawnie managed. She looked about as shorted out as I felt.

Gus glanced around at both of us and smiled. "Sure."

So that was how she could get along without a regular job. And that was why she had a Mellotron and a Dobro and stuff in her junk sheds. And that was how she could get rock concert tickets when they were sold out. But—

"But Gus," I blurted out, "who's your friend?"

She knew exactly what I meant, right away: that the person who wrote "The Friendship Song" should have some sort of special friend for life. Her smile widened and her nose got extra pink. "It was always just sort of a dream before," she said. "Now it's your father."

Rawnie's face lit up and she grinned like Miss America. She looked the way I felt. "Radical," she said.

"All *riiight!*" I agreed. Then I shut up, because of the look in Nico's eyes. He was trying to smile, but his voice was wistful and faraway when he said to Gus, "That's the way it's been for me. A dream."

Everybody in the room except him had something she'd always wanted and never gotten, and we all knew it. Gus walked over to his bed and touched his hand. "Don't give up on it," she said.

"I won't." Nico gazed up at her. "I did almost blow it, though. After Ty let me down."

"You were entitled to feel betrayed."

"I guess. But I was stupid. You know, it wasn't even so much that I really liked him. I just wanted somebody to hang my heart on, and I did it to him."

"Oh." Gus nodded at him. "I see. You gotta wait for the right person, kiddo."

"Yeah, I know. It wasn't even really Ty's fault. He was just being who he really is, and I had these ideas of him—us—and he shot them full of holes."

"Listen, keep some of those ideas. Keep the faith."

"I will. I am. I've got my act back together now."

"Okay." She blinked and seemed to realize that she barely knew him, so she backed off a little. "I don't mean to tell you what to do. We just came by to see if we could help."

"I think you already did." Nico turned his head, looking at Rawnie and me like somebody had just played a joke on him, the good kind, and he hadn't quite figured it out yet, but he knew it meant somebody liked him. There was a smile just starting at the corners of his mouth. "I'm not sure what's going on here, but I know you two. I dreamed about you."

I guess he could see we weren't surprised, but we didn't say much. He wasn't real strong yet, and we didn't want to wear him out with talking. We just said hi, and we told him our names, and Rawnie said, "I hope it was a good dream."

"The best. There was the most incredible band,

and you were fronting it, and Harper was playing the hottest ax I've ever heard. And you both sang, and every word was for me. You were doing it for me."

This didn't make much sense, yet it sort of did. I said, " 'The Friendship Song.' "

"Yes. And all through it I felt like I just wanted to die, you know? Because something I believed in was shot down in flames. But then after you were done I finally started to see, I understood. I could still believe. 'The Friendship Song' was still alive. It was just not in me right now. It was in you. In you two."

I looked at Rawnie and Rawnie looked at me, and I knew that for that moment we were standing right on the center of the circle that was eternity. Right on the hub of yang and yin, with lifetime after lifetime of black and white spinning through us. And then Rawnie opened her mouth and started to sing, and she hip-hopped and started to dance, she just had to, because outside in the street somebody was walking by with a boom box that was playing,

Hey, I remember when
We were desperadoes
You had a guitar on your back
And I had a gun in my hand
And when it came down to the end
You took the bullet they meant for me
And smiled 'cause you could see
I was gonna be okay
Friend. . . .